A Treasury of
Bedtime Stories

A Treasury of Bedtime Stories

More Than 40 Classic Tales for Sweet Dreams!

Edited by Althea L. Clinton
Illustrated by Eleanora Madsen and Fern Bisel Peat

FOR
YOUNG
READERS

First published in 1933 by The Saalfield Publishing Company

First Racehorse for Young Readers Edition 2017

Racehorse for Young Readers books may be purchased in bulk at special discounts for sales promotion, corporate gifts, fund-raising, or educational purposes. Special editions can also be created to specifications. For details, contact the Special Sales Department, Skyhorse Publishing, 307 West 36th Street, 11th Floor, New York, NY 10018 or info@skyhorsepublishing.com.

Racehorse for Young Readers™ is a pending trademark of Skyhorse Publishing, Inc.®, a Delaware corporation.

Visit our website at www.skyhorsepublishing.com.

10 9 8 7 6 5 4 3 2 1

Library of Congress Cataloging-in-Publication Data is available on file.

Print ISBN: 978-1-944686-07-9
Ebook ISBN: 978-1-944686-16-1

Jacket and color interior artwork by Eleanora Madsen
Black and white interior artwork by Fern Bisel Peat

Printed in China

CONTENTS

CONTENTS (Concluded)

COLOR ILLUSTRATIONS

Drakestail

DRAKESTAIL was very little. But tiny as he was, he had brains, for having begun with nothing he ended by amassing a hundred crowns.

Now the King of the country went one day in his own person to borrow his hoard. And, my word, Drakestail was not a little proud of having lent money to the King! But after the first and second year, seeing the King never even paid the interest, he became uneasy and resolved to go and see His Majesty.

So one fine morning Drakestail, very spruce and fresh, takes the road, singing:

"Quack, quack, quack,
  When shall I get my money back?"

He had not gone far when he met friend Fox.

"Good-morning, neighbor," says the friend. "Where are you off to so early?"

"I am going to the King for what he owes me."

"Oh! take me with thee!"

Drakestail said to himself: "One can't have too many friends." . . . . "I will," says he. "But going on all fours, you will soon be tired. Make yourself quite small, get into my throat—go into my gizzard, and I will carry you."

"Happy thought!" says friend Fox.

He takes bag and baggage, and, presto! is gone like a letter into the post. And Drakestail is off again, singing:

"Quack, quack, quack,
  When shall I get my money back?"

He had not gone far when he met his lady friend Ladder, leaning on her wall.

"Good-morning, my duckling," says the lady friend. "Whither away so bold?"

"I am going to the King for what he owes me."

"Oh! take me with thee!"

Drakestail said to himself: "One can't have too many friends." . . . . "I will," says he. "But with your wooden legs, you will soon be tired. Make yourself quite small, get into my throat—go into my gizzard, and I will carry you."

"Happy thought!" says my friend Ladder. And nimble, bag and baggage, goes to keep company with friend Fox. And "Quack, quack, quack," Drakestail is off again, singing.

A little farther he meets his sweetheart, my friend River.

"Thou, my cherub," says she, "whither so lonesome, with arching tail, on this muddy road?"

"I am going to the King for what he owes me."

"Oh! take me with thee!"

Drakestail said to himself: "One can't have too many friends." .... "I will," says he. "But you who sleep while you walk will soon be tired. Make yourself quite small, get into my throat—go into my gizzard, and I will carry you."

"Ah! happy thought!" says my friend River.

She takes bag and baggage, and glou, glou, glou, she takes her place between friend Fox and my friend Ladder. And "Quack, quack, quack," Drakestail is off again, singing as before.

A little farther on he meets comrade Wasp's-nest, maneuvering his wasps.

"Well, good-morning, friend Drakestail," said comrade Wasp's-nest. "Where are we bound for so spruce and fresh?"

"I am going to the King for what he owes me."

"Oh! take me with thee!" said comrade Wasp's-nest.

Drakestail said to himself: "One can't have too many friends." .... "I will," says he. "But with your battalion to drag along, you will soon be tired. Make yourself quite small, get into my throat—go into my gizzard, and I will carry you."

"By Jove! that's a good idea!" says comrade Wasp's-nest.

And left file! he takes the same road to join the others with all his party. And Drakestail is off again, singing:

"Quack, quack, quack,
When shall I get my money back?"

He arrived thus at the capital, and threaded his way straight up High Street till he came to the King's palace.

He strikes with the knocker: "Toc, toc!"

"Who is there?" asks the porter, putting his head out of the wicket.

"'Tis I, Drakestail. I wish to speak to the King."

"Speak to the King! That's easily said! The King is dining, and will not be disturbed."

"Tell him that it is I, and I have come he well knows why."

The porter shuts his wicket and goes up to say it to the King, who was just sitting down to dinner with a napkin round his neck, and all his ministers.

"Good, good!" said the King, laughing. "I know what it is! Make him come in, and put him with the turkeys and chickens."

The porter descends.

"Have the goodness to enter."

"Good!" says Drakestail to himself. "I shall now see how they eat at Court."

"This way, this way," says the porter. "One step farther. . . . . . There, there you are!"

"How? what? in the poultry yard?"

Fancy how vexed Drakestail was!

"Ah! so that's it," says he. "Wait! I will compel you to receive me.

"Quack, quack, quack,
  When shall I get my money back?"

But turkeys and chickens are creatures who don't like those that are not as themselves. When they saw the newcomer, they rushed at him all together to overwhelm him with pecks.

"I am lost!" said Drakestail to himself, when by good luck he remembered his comrade, friend Fox, and he cries:

"Reynard, Reynard, come out of your earth,
  Or Drakestail's life is of little worth."

Then friend Fox, who was only waiting for these words, hastens out, throws himself on the wicked fowls, and quick! quack! he tears them to pieces. And Drakestail, quite content, began to sing again,

"Quack, quack, quack,
  When shall I get my money back?"

When the King who was still at the table heard this refrain, he was terribly annoyed and ordered them to throw this tail of a drake into the well.

And it was done as he commanded.

Drakestail was in despair of getting himself out of such a deep hole, when he remembered his lady friend, the Ladder.

"Ladder, Ladder, come out of thy hold,
  Or Drakestail's days will soon be told."

My friend Ladder, who was only waiting for these words, hastens out, and leans her two arms on the edge of the well. Then Drakestail climbs nimbly on her back, and hop! he is in the yard, where he begins to sing louder than ever.

When the King, who was still at table and laughing at the trick he had played his creditor, heard him again reclaiming his money, he became livid with rage. He commanded that the furnace should be heated, and this tail of a drake thrown into it.

The furnace was soon hot, but this time Drakestail was not so afraid; he counted on his sweetheart, my friend River.

"River, River, outward flow,
  Or to death Drakestail must go."

My friend River hastens out, and errouf! throws herself into the furnace which

she floods. After that she flowed growling into the hall of the palace.

And Drakestail, quite content, begins to swim, singing deafeningly:

"Quack, quack, quack,
When shall I get my money back?"

The King was still at table, and thought himself quite sure of his game; but when he heard Drakestail singing again, he became furious and got up from table, brandishing his fists.

"Bring him here, and I'll cut his throat! Bring him here quick!" cried he.

Quickly two footmen ran to fetch Drakestail.

"At last," said the poor chap, going up the great stairs, "they have decided to receive me."

Imagine his terror when on entering he sees the King as red as a turkey cock, and all his ministers attending him standing sword in hand. He thought this time it was all up with him. Happily he remembered that there was still one remaining friend, and he cried with dying accents:

"Wasp's-nest, Wasp's-nest, make a sally,
Or Drakestail nevermore may rally."

Hereupon the scene changes.

"Bs, bs, bayonet them!" The brave Wasp's-nest rushes out with all his wasps. They threw themselves on the infuriated King and his ministers, and stung them so fiercely in the face that they lost their heads, and not knowing where to hide themselves, they all jumped pell-mell from the window and broke their necks on the pavement.

Behold Drakestail much astonished, all alone in the big saloon and master of the field. He could not get over it.

Nevertheless, he remembered shortly why he had come to the palace, and he set to work to hunt for his dear money. But in vain he rummaged in all the drawers. He found nothing. And ferreting thus from room to room, he came at last to the one with the throne in it, and feeling fatigued, he sat himself down on it to think over his adventure.

In the meanwhile the people had found their King and his ministers on the pavement with their feet in the air, and they had gone into the palace to learn how it had occurred.

On entering the throne-room, when the crowd saw that there was already someone on the royal seat, they broke out in cries of surprise and joy:

"The King is dead, long live the King!
Heaven has sent us down this thing."

They ran and took the crown off the head of the deceased, and placed it on that of Drakestail, whom it fitted like wax.

Thus he became King.

"And now," said he, after the ceremony, "ladies and gentlemen, let's go to supper. I am so hungry!"

—Adapted from the French.

14

The Magpie's Nest

ONCE upon a time when pigs spoke rhyme and ducks went quack, quack, quack, O! all the birds came to the magpie and asked her to teach them how to build nests. For the magpie is the cleverest bird of all at building nests. So she put all the birds round her and began to show them how to do it. First of all she took some mud and made a sort of round cake with it.

"Oh, that's how it's done," said the thrush; and away it flew, and so that's how thrushes build their nests.

Then the magpie took some twigs and arranged them round in the mud.

"Now I know all about it," said the blackbird, and off he flew; and that's how the blackbirds make their nests to this very day.

Then the magpie put another layer of mud over the twigs.

"Oh, that's quite obvious," said the wise owl, and away it flew; and owls have never made better nests since.

After this the magpie took some twigs and twined them round the outside.

"The very thing!" said the sparrow, and off he went; so sparrows make rather slovenly nests to this day.

Well, then Madge Magpie took some feathers and stuff and lined the nest very comfortably with it.

"That suits me," cried the starling, and off it flew; and very comfortable nests have starlings.

So it went on, every bird taking away some knowledge of how to build nests, but none of them waiting to the end. Meanwhile Madge Magpie went on working and working without looking up till the only bird that remained was the turtle-dove, and it hadn't paid any attention all along, but only kept repeating its silly cry: "Take two, Taffy, take two-o-o-o."

At last the magpie heard this just as she was putting a twig across. So she said: "One's enough."

But the turtle-dove kept on saying: "Take two, Taffy, take two-o-o-o."

Then the magpie got angry and said: "One's enough, I tell you!"

Still the turtle-dove cried: "Take two, Taffy, take two-o-o-o."

At last the magpie looked up and saw nobody near her but the silly turtle-dove, and then she got rarely angry and flew away and refused to tell the birds how to build nests again. And that is why different birds build their nests differently.

The Tale of Peter Rabbit

ONCE upon a time there were four little rabbits, and their names were Flopsy, Mopsy, Cotton-tail and Peter. They lived with their mother in a sand-bank, underneath the root of a very big fir tree.

"Now, my dears," said old Mrs. Rabbit one morning, "you may go into the fields or down the lane, but don't go into Mr. McGregor's garden. Your father had an accident there; he was put in a pie by Mrs. McGregor. Now run along and don't get into mischief. I am going out."

Then old Mrs. Rabbit took a basket and her umbrella and went through the wood to the baker's. She bought a loaf of brown bread and five currant buns.

Flopsy, Mopsy and Cotton-tail, who were good little bunnies, went down the lane together to gather blackberries. But Peter, who was very naughty, ran straight away to Mr. McGregor's garden and squeezed under the gate! First he ate some lettuces and some French beans; and then he ate some radishes; and then, feeling rather sick, he went to look for some parsley. But round the end of a cucumber frame, whom should he meet but Mr. McGregor!

Mr. McGregor was on his hands and knees planting out young cabbages, but he jumped up and ran after Peter, waving a rake and calling out "Stop thief!"

Peter was most dreadfully frightened; he rushed all over the garden, for he had forgotten the way back to the gate. He lost one shoe among the cabbages, and the other amongst the potatoes.

After losing them, he ran on four legs and went faster, so that I think he might have got away altogether if he had not unfortunately run into a gooseberry net and got caught by the large buttons on his jacket. It was a blue jacket with brass buttons, quite new. Peter gave himself up for lost and shed big tears; but his sobs were overheard by some friendly sparrows who flew to him in great excitement and implored him to exert himself.

Mr. McGregor came up with a sieve which he intended to pop on the top of Peter, but Peter wriggled out just in time, leaving his jacket behind him.

He rushed into the tool shed and—jumped into a can. It would have been a beautiful thing to hide in, if it had not had so much water in it. Mr. McGregor was quite sure that Peter was somewhere in the tool shed, perhaps hidden underneath a flower-pot. He began to turn them over carefully, looking under each.

Presently Peter sneezed "Kertyschoo!"

Mr. McGregor was after him in no time, and tried to put his foot upon Peter, who jumped out of a window, upsetting three plants. The window was too small for Mr. McGregor, and he was tired of running after Peter. He went back to his work.

Peter sat down to rest; he was out of breath and trembling with fright, and he had not the least idea which way to go. Also he was very damp with sitting in that can.

After a time he began to wander about, going lippity—lippity—not very fast and

A Color Illustration *(over)*

Peter, who was very naughty, ran straight away to Mr. McGregor's garden.

looking all around. He found a door in a wall; but it was locked and there was no room for a fat little rabbit to squeeze underneath.

An old mouse was running in and out over the stone doorstep, carrying peas and beans to her family in the wood. Peter asked her the way to the gate but she had such a large pea in her mouth she could not answer. She only shook her head at him.

Peter began to cry.

Then he tried to find his way straight across the garden, but he became more and more puzzled. Presently he came to a pond where Mr. McGregor filled his water-cans. A white cat was staring at some gold-fish; she sat very, very still, but now and then the tip of her tail twitched as if it were alive. Peter thought it best to go away without speaking to her. He had heard about cats from his cousin, little Benjamin Bunny.

He went back towards the tool shed, but suddenly, quite close to him, he heard the noise of a hoe—scr-r-ritch, scratch, scratch, scritch. Peter scuttered underneath the bushes, but presently as nothing happened, he came out and climbed upon a wheelbarrow, and peeped over.

The first thing he saw was Mr. McGregor hoeing onions. His back was turned towards Peter and beyond him was the gate!

Peter got down very quietly off the wheelbarrow and started running as fast as he could go, along a straight walk behind some black currant bushes. Mr. McGregor caught sight of him at the corner, but Peter did not care. He slipped underneath the gate and was safe at last in the wood outside the garden.

Mr. McGregor hung up the little jacket and the shoes for a scarecrow to frighten the blackbirds.

Peter never stopped running or looked behind him till he got home to the big fir tree. He was so tired that he flopped down upon the nice soft sand on the floor of the rabbit hole, and shut his eyes. His mother was busy

cooking; she wondered what he had done with his clothes. It was the second little jacket and pair of shoes that Peter had lost in a fortnight!

I am sorry to say that Peter was not very well during the evening. His mother put him to bed and made some camomile tea; and she gave a dose of it to Peter! "One teaspoonful to be taken at bedtime." But—Flopsy, Mopsy and Cotton-tail had bread and milk and blackberries for supper.

—*Beatrix Potter.*

Dame Wiggins of Lee
and Her Seven Wonderful Cats

DAME WIGGINS of Lee
    Was a worthy old soul
As e'er threaded a nee-
dle, or washed in a bowl;
She held mice and rats
In such antipath*ee*,
That seven fine cats
Kept Dame Wiggins of Lee.

The rats and mice scared
By this fierce-whiskered crew,
The poor seven cats
Soon had nothing to do;
So, as anyone idle
She ne'er loved to see,
She sent them to school,
Did Dame Wiggins of Lee.

But soon she grew tired
Of living alone;
So she sent for her cats
From school to come home.
Each rowing a wherry,
Returning you see:
The frolic made merry
Dame Wiggins of Lee.

The Dame was quite pleased
And ran out to market;
When she came back
They were mending the carpet.
The needle each handled
As brisk as a bee.
"Well done, my good cats,"
Said Dame Wiggins of Lee.

To give them a treat,
She ran out for some rice;
When she came back,
They were skating on ice.
"I shall soon see one down,
Aye, perhaps two or three,
I'll bet half-a-crown,"
Said Dame Wiggins of Lee.

They called the next day
On the tomtit and sparrow,
And wheeled a poor sick lamb
Home in a barrow.
"You shall all have some sprats
For your humanit*ee*,
My seven good cats,"
Said Dame Wiggins of Lee.

While she ran to the field,
To look for its dam,
They were warming the bed
For the poor sick lamb:
They turned up the clothes
All as neat as could be.
"I shall ne'er want a nurse,"
Said Dame Wiggins of Lee.

She wished them good-night,
And went up to bed:
When, lo! in the morning
The cats were all fled.
But soon—what a fuss!
"Where can they all be?
Here, pussy, puss, puss!"
Cried Dame Wiggins of Lee.

The Dame's heart was nigh broke,
So she sat down to weep,
When she saw them come back,
Each riding a sheep:
She fondled and patted
Each purring tomm*ee*:
"Ah! welcome, my dears,"
Said Dame Wiggins of Lee.

The Dame was unable
Her pleasure to smother,
To see the sick lamb
Jump up to its mother.
In spite of the gout,
And a pain in her knee,
She went dancing about,
Did Dame Wiggins of Lee.

The Farmer soon heard
Where his sheep went astray,
And arrived at Dame's door
With his faithful dog Tray.
He knocked with his crook,
And the stranger to see,
Out the window did look
Dame Wiggins of Lee.

For their kindness he had them
All drawn by his team;
And gave them some field-mice
And raspberry cream.
Said he, "All my stock
You shall presently see,
For I *know* the cats
Of Dame Wiggins of Lee."

He sent his maid out
For some muffins and crumpets;
And when he turned round
They were blowing of trumpets.
Said he, "I suppose
She's as deaf as can be,
Or this ne'er could be borne
By Dame Wiggins of Lee."

To show them his poultry,
He turned them all loose,
Then each nimbly leaped
On the back of a goose,
Which frightened them so
That they ran to the sea,
And half-drowned the poor cats
Of Dame Wiggins of Lee.

For the care of his lamb
And their comical pranks,
He gave them a ham
And abundance of thanks.
"I wish you good-day,
My fine fellows," said he;
"My compliments, pray,
To Dame Wiggins of Lee."

You see them arrived
At their Dame's welcome door;
They show her their presents,
And all their good store.
"Now come in to supper,
And sit down with me;
All welcome once more,"
Cried Dame Wiggins of Lee.

—*Old Rhyme.*

The Teeny-Tiny Woman

ONCE upon a time there was a teeny-tiny woman who lived in a teeny-tiny house in a teeny-tiny village. Now, one day this teeny-tiny woman put on her teeny-tiny bonnet, and went out of her teeny-tiny house to take a teeny-tiny walk.

And when this teeny-tiny woman had gone a teeny-tiny way, she came to a teeny-tiny gate; so the teeny-tiny woman opened the teeny-tiny gate, and went into a teeny-tiny churchyard.

And when this teeny-tiny woman had got into the teeny-tiny churchyard, she saw a teeny-tiny bone on a teeny-tiny grave, and the teeny-tiny woman said to her teeny-tiny self, "This teeny-tiny bone will make me some teeny-tiny soup for my teeny-tiny supper." So the teeny-tiny woman put the teeny-tiny bone into her teeny-tiny pocket, and went home to her teeny-tiny house.

Now when the teeny-tiny woman got home to her teeny-tiny house, she was a teeny-tiny bit tired; so she put the teeny-tiny bone into her teeny-tiny cupboard, and went up her teeny-tiny stairs to her teeny-tiny bed. And when this teeny-tiny woman had been to sleep a teeny-tiny time, she was awakened by a teeny-tiny voice from the teeny-tiny cupboard, which said:

"GIVE ME MY BONE!"

And this teeny-tiny woman was a teeny-tiny frightened, so she hid her teeny-tiny head under the teeny-tiny clothes and went to sleep again. And when she had been to sleep again a teeny-tiny time, the teeny-tiny voice again cried out from the teeny-tiny cupboard a teeny-tiny louder:

"GIVE ME MY BONE!"

This made the teeny-tiny woman a teeny-tiny more frightened, so she hid her teeny-tiny head a teeny-tiny further under the teeny-tiny clothes. And when the teeny-tiny woman had been to sleep again a teeny-tiny time, the teeny-tiny voice from the teeny-tiny cupboard said again a teeny-tiny louder:

"GIVE ME MY BONE!"

And this teeny-tiny woman was a teeny-tiny bit more frightened, but she put her teeny-tiny head out of the teeny-tiny clothes, and said in her loudest teeny-tiny voice, "TAKE IT!"

20

Hansel and Gretel

ONCE upon a time near a great forest there lived a poor wood-cutter. He had two children. The boy was called Hansel and the girl was called Gretel. Their own mother had died and the wood-cutter had married a new wife to take care of them.

There had always been little enough in the cottage to live on, but when a famine came to the land, the wood-cutter could not get even bread for his family. One night as he tossed about on his bed he groaned to his wife: "How are we to feed our poor children when we have nothing even for ourselves? Whatever is to become of us?"

"I'll tell you, husband," replied the woman. "Early tomorrow morning we will take the children deep into the great forest. There we will build a fire for them, give each a piece of bread and then go on to our work and leave them alone. They will not be able to find their way home and thus we shall be rid of them."

"No, wife," said the wood-cutter, "I won't do that. How could I leave Hansel and Gretel alone in the forest? The wild beasts would soon come and devour them!"

"Fool!" exclaimed the woman. "Then all four of us must die of hunger. You may just as well go now and make our coffins." She left him no peace until he said he would do as she wished.

Now Hansel and Gretel had been unable to sleep because they were too hungry, and so they had heard all this talk between their father and his wife. "Now all is over with us!" wept Gretel bitterly.

"No, no!" Hansel assured her. "Don't fret so, Gretel. I will surely find some way out of our trouble."

They waited until the old people had fallen asleep. Then Hansel got out of bed, slipped on his little coat, opened the door quietly and stole out of doors. The moon was shining so brightly that the little white pebbles that lay thick in front of the cottage glittered like bits of silver. Hansel bent down and filled one pocket after another with them. Then he crept silently back into the cottage, and as he lay down to sleep, he whispered to his sister, "Go to sleep, little sister, for surely God will not forsake us."

The next morning the woman did not wait until the sun was up to come to the children's bedside. "Get up, lazy things!" she said, "we are all going to the forest to fetch wood," and handing each a little piece of bread, she added: "There is your dinner. Don't eat it before noon, for you'll get nothing more."

Gretel took the bread under her apron, for Hansel had the white stones in his pockets, and the four set out to the forest.

When they had been walking a short time, Hansel stopped, turned and looked back at the cottage. This he did again and again. Finally his father saw him and said, "Hansel, why are you lagging behind? And why gaze so at the path you have just traveled? Take care or you will stumble and fall."

"Oh, father," replied Hansel, "I am looking back at my little white kitten. It

21

is sitting on the roof of the cottage and waving me a farewell."

"Fool!" exclaimed the woman. "That is not your kitten. It's the morning sun shining on the chimney."

But Hansel had not been looking back at the cat at all; he had been dropping the white pebbles out of his pocket on the path through the forest.

When they reached the middle of the forest, the father said, "Children, hurry and fetch brushwood. I'll build a fire and you will not feel cold."

Hansel and Gretel gathered a great heap until the pile was like a small hill. As the flames leaped high above it, the woman said, "Now lie down and rest near the fire, while your father and I go to our work. When we have finished, we will come and fetch you back."

Hansel and Gretel sat down beside the fire and when noon came ate their bread. At last they fell asleep. It was black night when they awoke. Gretel began to cry, but Hansel comforted her with, "When the moon rises, we will soon find our way back."

And when the full moon had risen, they followed the white pebbles which shone like bright silver coins in the moonlight. By break of day they came to their father's house. The woman answered their knock and said, "You naughty children, we thought you were never coming back at all!"

But the father was glad, for it had cut his heart deep to leave his children in the forest.

Not long after this there was another great famine in the land, and the two children heard the woman say to their father one night, "We have only a half loaf left. The children must go. This time we will lead them farther into the wood," and she gave him no peace until he had consented.

The children were awake and had heard the plan, so after the old people were sound asleep, Hansel got up to gather pebbles again. But this time the woman had barred the door and Hansel could not get out. He went back to his sister and said, "Do not cry, Gretel. Go to sleep. The good God will surely help us."

A Color Illustration *(over)*

    The door opened and out crept
    a very old, old woman on crutches.

Early the next morning the woman came and gave each a bit of bread—smaller than before.

On the way to the forest, Hansel crumbled his bread in his pocket, and often threw a morsel on the ground. At last the father asked, "Hansel, why do you stop so often and look around?"

"I am looking at my little pigeon sitting on the roof and wanting to say good-bye to me."

"Goose!" exclaimed the woman. "That is not your pigeon. It's the morning sun shining on the chimney."

They led the children deep into the forest, made a great fire and then the woman said, "Sit here, and when you are tired you may sleep a little. When our wood is cut we will fetch you away."

Noon came and Gretel shared her little piece of bread with Hansel, and then they fell asleep. When they woke it was black night, and Gretel wept with fright. Hansel comforted her, saying, "Gretel, when the moon rises we shall see the crumbs I scattered and they will show us the way home."

When the moon rose, they set out, but the birds of the forest had picked up all the crumbs.

They walked all that night and all the following day, but did not get out of the forest. When they were so tired they could walk no more, they lay down and fell asleep under a tree.

Three days afterward they saw a beautiful snow-white bird. They followed it until they reached a little house built of bread and covered with cakes, with windows of clear sugar.

"I will eat the roof and you can eat some of the windows," said Hansel.

Then a soft voice from the little house cried:

"Nibble, nibble, gnaw,
  Who is nibbling at my little house?"
The children answered:
  "The wind, the wind, the wind of heaven!"
and went on eating.

The door opened and out crept a very old, old woman on crutches.

"Oh, you dear children! Who has brought you here? Do come in and stay with me," and she led them into her little house. She set before them milk and pancakes with sugar, and apples and nuts, too. Then she put them to bed between clean linen.

23

The old hag only pretended to be kind. In truth she was a wicked witch, and early the next morning when she saw the children still sleeping, she muttered, "They will make a dainty mouthful!" Then she seized Hansel, and locked him in a stable.

Every morning the witch crept to the stable and cried, "Hansel, stretch out your finger that I may feel if you soon will be fat enough to eat."

Hansel, however, stretched out a little bone to her, and the old hag having dim eyes wondered why he did not grow fat.

When four weeks had gone by, she could wait no longer. "Come, Gretel," she cried, "bring some water. Let Hansel be fat or lean, tomorrow I will cook him."

"Dear God, help us!" cried Gretel as she obeyed.

Early the next morning Gretel had to go out and hang up the kettle and light the fire.

"We will bake first," said the old woman. "I have heated the oven and the dough is ready."

She pushed poor Gretel to the oven and said, "Creep in and see if it is heated."

But Gretel knew what she meant to do, so she said, "How do you get in?"

"Goose! The door is big enough. Just look, I can get in myself!" And she crept in.

Gretel gave her a push that sent her far into it, and shut the iron door tight.

Then Gretel ran quick as lightning to the stable and cried, "Hansel, Hansel, we are free! The old witch is dead!"

And now as they had no reason to fear, they went into the witch's house. In every corner stood chests all full of jewels and pearls.

"These are far better than pebbles," said Hansel as he filled his pockets, and Gretel filled her apron, too. "Now we will go away, that we may get out of the witch's forest."

They walked for hours, and came at last to a great lake. "We cannot get across," said Hansel. "Look, Gretel, there is neither foot-plank nor bridge."

"And no ferry-boat, either," answered Gretel. "But I see a white duck swimming there. If I ask, she will help us over." Then she cried:

"Little duck, little duck, dost thou see
Hansel and Gretel are waiting for thee?
There's never a plank nor a bridge in sight;
Take us across on thy back so white."

The duck came to them, and Hansel told Gretel to get on the duck's back by his side.

"Oh, no!" replied Gretel. "We will be too heavy for the little duck. She shall take you across and then come and take me."

When they were safely over, they saw their father's house afar off. Then they began to run and rushed in, throwing themselves into his arms. How glad he was, for he had not had one happy hour since he had left his children in the deep forest. The woman, however, had died. Gretel emptied her apron until pearls and precious jewels rolled around the room, while Hansel tossed one handful after another out of his pockets to do his share.

Then all care was at an end, and the three—father, Hansel and Gretel—lived happily ever after.

—*Adapted from the Brothers Grimm.*

The Gingerbread Boy

ONCE upon a time a little old woman and a little old man lived in a little old house. You will know they were lonely when I tell you there was no little boy, no little girl in that little old house.

One day the little old woman said to herself, "I am going to make a gingerbread boy. Then we'll not be so lonely."

That is how it came that she mixed some gingerbread dough and rolled it out with unusual care. She took her round cooky cutter and cut out a head. Then she took a larger, oval cooky cutter and cut out the body. Two long pieces of dough made a fine pair of arms, and two sturdy legs were added too.

"He must have some clothes," thought the little old woman, and she put six round, flat black currants down the front of his brown jacket.

Two tiny dots of sugar frosting just in the right places made his eyes, while a lump of sugar made his pug of a nose. Oh, the little woman used great care as she put on the narrow line of sugar frosting that made his mouth. She wanted a smiling boy in her house, you see.

At last she lifted him gently and popped him into the oven.

Now it was hot in the little old woman's oven—much too hot for the gingerbread boy, so he called out, "Open the door! I want to get out!" But the little old woman never heard him, for she was putting away her baking things with a great noise and clatter.

The oven grew hotter—much hotter, and the gingerbread boy called louder: "Open the door! I want to get out, I do!" But by this time the little old woman was singing happily as she went from cupboard

to table, for she was thinking, "Now I shall have a little boy all my own!"

The oven grew hotter — oh, very much hotter, and the gingerbread boy beat on the door. Then the little old woman sniffed the air and ran to the oven, saying, "Dearie me! I mustn't let my gingerbread burn!" She threw open the door and the gingerbread boy jumped onto the floor and ran straight for the door. He waved his arms and called back over his shoulder:

> "I am the gingerbread boy, I am, I am;
> I can run from you, I can, I can!"

The little old woman picked up her skirts and ran after the gingerbread boy as fast as she could run, but she couldn't catch him.

The little old man was making a garden and looked up just as the gingerbread boy ran out the gate, the little old woman close behind.

The gingerbread boy waved his arms and called back over his shoulder to the little old man:

> "I am the gingerbread boy, I am, I am;
> I can run from you, I can, I can!
> I ran away from a little old woman,
> And I can run from you, I can, I can!"

The little old man dropped his rake and ran after the gingerbread boy as fast as he could run, but he couldn't catch him.

On, on ran the gingerbread boy until he came to a field where men were swinging great scythes as they cut the sweet hay. They looked up and saw the gingerbread boy, the little old woman and the little old man running across the field.

The gingerbread boy waved his arms and called back over his shoulder to the mowers:

> "I am the gingerbread boy, I am, I am;
> I can run from you, I can, I can!
> I ran away from a little old woman,
> A little old man,
> And I can run from you, I can, I can!"

The mowers dropped their scythes and ran after the gingerbread boy as fast as they could run, but they couldn't catch him.

On, on ran the gingerbread boy until he came to a great barn where the men were threshing the grain. They looked up and saw the gingerbread boy, the little old woman, the little old man and the mowers all running past the barn.

The gingerbread boy waved his arms and called back over his shoulder:

> "I am the gingerbread boy, I am, I am;
> I can run from you, I can, I can!
> I ran away from a little old woman,
> A little old man,
> A field full of mowers,
> And I can run from you, I can, I can!"

The threshers dropped their flails and ran after the gingerbread boy as fast as they could run, but they couldn't catch him.

On, on ran the gingerbread boy until he came to a pasture where an old red cow was chewing her cud.

The gingerbread boy waved his arms and called back over his shoulder to the old red cow:

> "I am the gingerbread boy, I am, I am;
> I can run from you, I can, I can!
> I ran away from a little old woman,
> A little old man,
> A field full of mowers,
> A barn full of threshers,
> And I can run from you, I can, I can!"

The old red cow rolled her big soft eyes and said, "Moo! Moo!" (which meant "No! No!") and ran after the gingerbread boy as fast as she could run, but she couldn't catch him.

On, on ran the gingerbread boy until he met a big, fat pig.

The gingerbread boy waved his arms and called back over his shoulder to the pig:

A Color Illustration *(over)*

The old woman threw open the oven door,
and the gingerbread boy jumped out.

"I am the gingerbread boy, I am, I am;
I can run from you, I can, I can!
I ran away from a little old woman,
A little old man,
A field full of mowers,
A barn full of threshers,
An old red cow,
And I can run from you, I can, I can!"

The pig went "Ouf! Ouf!" (which meant "No! No!") and ran after the gingerbread boy as fast as he could run, but he couldn't catch him.

On, on ran the gingerbread boy far, far into the woods until he saw a sly old fox under the tree. As the fox had his eyes half closed, the gingerbread boy thought he was asleep, so he ran close to him, waved his arms just as he had to the pig, and called out:

"I am the gingerbread boy, I am, I am;
I can run from you, I can, I can!
I ran away from a little old woman,
A little old man,
A field full of mowers,
A barn full of threshers,
An old red cow,
A big fat pig,
And I can run from you, I can, I can!"

Then the sly old fox opened his eyes, and he opened his mouth, too—and grabbed the gingerbread boy by the leg.

One bite, and the fox found he liked the gingerbread boy very well. He ate all the leg, smacking his lips and saying, "Um!" as he licked his chops.

The gingerbread boy wiped a tear away as he wailed: "One leg all gone!"

Then the fox ate the other leg, smacking his lips and saying, "Um-m!" as he licked his chops.

The gingerbread boy wiped a tear away as he wailed: "Two legs all gone!"

Then the fox began to eat the gingerbread boy's body, smacking his lips and saying, "Um-m-m!" as he licked his chops.

The gingerbread boy wiped a tear away as he wailed: "Half gone!"

Then the fox ate one of the gingerbread boy's arms, smacking his lips and saying, "Um-m-m-m!" as he licked his chops.

The gingerbread boy wiped a tear away as he wailed: "One arm all gone!"

Then the fox ate the other arm, smacking his lips and saying, "Um-m-m-m-m!" as he licked his chops.

The gingerbread boy let the tears roll down his face—you see he could do nothing else as he weakly wailed: "Two arms all gone!"

Then the fox ate the gingerbread boy's head with a great gulp, while a far-away voice wailed: "All gone!"

And that was the last of the Gingerbread Boy!

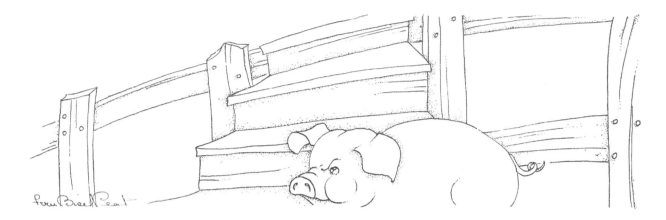

The Old Woman and Her Pig

AN OLD woman was sweeping her house, and she found a little crooked sixpence. "What," said she, "shall I do with this little sixpence? I will go to market, and buy me a pig."

As she was coming home, she came to a stile; but the pig wouldn't get over the stile.

She went a little further, and she met a dog. So she said: "Dog! dog! bite pig; pig won't get over the stile; and I shan't get home to-night." But the dog would not.

She went a little further, and she met a stick. So she said: "Stick! stick! beat dog; dog won't bite pig; pig won't get over the stile; and I shan't get home tonight." But the stick would not.

She went a little further, and she met a fire. So she said: "Fire! fire! burn stick; stick won't beat dog; dog won't bite pig; pig won't get over the stile; and I shan't get home tonight." But the fire would not.

She went a little further, and she met some water. So she said: "Water! water! quench fire; fire won't burn stick; stick won't beat dog; dog won't bite pig; pig won't get over the stile; and I shan't get home to-night." But the water would not.

She went a little further, and she met an ox. So she said: "Ox! ox! drink water; water won't quench fire; fire won't burn stick; stick won't beat dog; dog won't bite pig; pig won't get over the stile; and I shan't get home tonight." But the ox would not.

She went a little further, and she met a butcher. So she said: "Butcher! butcher! kill ox; ox won't drink water; water won't quench fire; fire won't burn stick; stick won't beat dog; dog won't bite pig; pig won't get over the stile; and I shan't get home tonight." But the butcher would not.

She went a little further, and she met a rope. So she said: "Rope! rope! hang butcher; butcher won't kill ox; ox won't drink water; water won't quench fire; fire won't burn stick; stick won't beat dog; dog won't bite pig; pig won't get over the stile; and I shan't get home tonight." But the rope would not.

She went a little further, and she met a rat. So she said: "Rat! rat! gnaw rope;

rope won't hang butcher; butcher won't kill ox; ox won't drink water; water won't quench fire; fire won't burn stick; stick won't beat dog; dog won't bite pig; pig won't get over the stile; and I shan't get home to-night." But the rat would not.

She went a little further, and she met a cat. So she said: "Cat! cat! kill rat; rat won't gnaw rope; rope won't hang butcher; butcher won't kill ox; ox won't drink water; water won't quench fire; fire won't burn stick; stick won't beat dog; dog won't bite pig; pig won't get over the stile; and I shan't get home tonight."

But the cat said to her, "If you will go to yonder cow, and fetch me a saucer of milk, I will kill the rat." So away went the old woman to the cow.

But the cow said to her: "If you will go to yonder hay-stack, and fetch me a handful of hay, I'll give you the milk." So away went the old woman to the hay-stack; and she brought the hay to the cow.

As soon as the cow had eaten the hay, she gave the old woman the milk; and away she went with it in a saucer to the cat.

As soon as the cat had lapped up the milk, the cat began to kill the rat; the rat began to gnaw the rope; the rope began to hang the butcher; the butcher began to kill the ox; the ox began to drink the water; the water began to quench the fire; the fire began to burn the stick; the stick began to beat the dog; the dog began to bite the pig; the pig in a fright jumped over the stile; and so the old woman got home that night.

—*From the English.*

Five Little Chickens

SAID the first little chicken
　With a queer little squirm,
"Oh, I wish I could find
　A fat little worm!"

Said the next little chicken
　With an odd little shrug,
"Oh, I wish I could find
　A good little bug!"

Said the third little chicken
　With a sharp little squeal,
"Oh, I wish I could find
　Some nice yellow meal!"

Said the fourth little chicken
　With a shake of her head,
"Oh, I wish I could find
　A small crumb of bread!"

Said the fifth little chicken
　As she looked all around,
"Oh, I wish I could find
　Any food on the ground!"

"Now, see here," said the mother
　From the green garden patch,
"If you want any breakfast,
　You must come and scratch."

—*Old Verse.*

Sleeping Beauty

ONCE upon a time there lived a king and queen who had no children, and this they lamented very much. But one day, as the queen was walking by the side of the river, a little fish lifted its head out of the water and said, "Your wish shall be fulfilled and you shall have a daughter."

What the little fish had foretold soon came to pass; and the queen had a little girl who was so very beautiful that the king could not cease looking on her for joy, and determined to hold a great feast. So he invited not only his relations, friends, and neighbors, but also the fairies, that they might be kind and good to his little daughter.

Now there were thirteen fairies in his kingdom, and he had only twelve golden dishes for them to eat out of, so that he was obliged to leave one of the fairies without an invitation. The rest came, and after the feast was over they gave all their best gifts to the little princess. One gave her virtue, another beauty, another riches, and so on till she had all that was excellent in the world.

When eleven had done blessing her, the thirteenth, who had not been invited and was very angry on that account, came in and determined to take her revenge. So she cried out, "The king's daughter shall in her fifteenth year be wounded by a spindle and fall down dead." Then the twelfth, who had not given her gift, came forward and said that the bad wish must be fulfilled, but that she could soften it and that the king's daughter should not die, but fall asleep for a hundred years.

But the king hoped to save his dear child from the threatened evil and ordered that all the spindles in the kingdom should be

bought and destroyed. All the fairies' gifts were in the meantime fulfilled; for the princess was so beautiful and well-behaved and amiable and wise that everyone who knew her loved her.

Now it happened that on the very day she was fifteen years old the king and queen were not at home, and she was left alone in the palace. So she roamed about by herself and looked at all the rooms and chambers, until at last she came to an old tower, to which there was a narrow staircase ending with a little door. In the door there was a golden key and when she turned it, the door sprang open and there sat an old lady spinning away very busily.

"Why, how now, good mother," said the princess, "what are you doing there?"

"Spinning," said the old lady, and nodded her head.

"How prettily that little thing turns round!" said the princess, and took the spindle and began to spin. But scarcely had she touched it before the prophecy was fulfilled and she fell down on the ground.

However, she was not dead but had only fallen into a deep sleep; and the king and the queen, who just then came home, and all their court fell asleep too. The horses slept in the stables, the dogs in the yard, the pigeons on the housetop, and the flies on the walls. Even the fire on the hearth left off blazing and went to sleep; and the meat that was roasting stood still; and the cook, who was at that moment pulling the kitchen-boy by the hair to give him a box on the ear for something he had done amiss, let him go, and both fell asleep. Everything stood still, and slept soundly.

A high hedge of thorns soon grew around the palace. Every year it became higher and thicker, until at last the whole palace was surrounded and hidden so that not even the roof or the chimneys could be seen.

But there went a report through all the land of the beautiful sleeping Briar Rose, for thus was the king's daughter called; so that from time to time several kings' sons came and tried to break through the thicket into the palace.

This they could never do, for the thorns and bushes laid hold of them as it were with hands, and there they stuck fast and died miserably.

After many, many years there came another king's son into that land, and an old man told him the story of the thicket of thorns and how a beautiful palace stood behind it, in which was a wondrous princess called Briar Rose, asleep with all her court. He told, too, how he had heard from his grandfather that many, many princes had come and had tried to break through the thicket but had stuck fast and died.

Then the young prince said, "All this shall not frighten me; I will go and see Briar Rose."

The old man tried to dissuade him, but he persisted in going.

Now that very day were the hundred years completed; and as the prince came to the thicket, he saw nothing but beautiful flowering shrubs, through which he passed with ease, and they closed after him as firm as ever.

Then he came at last to the palace, and there in the yard lay the dogs asleep, and the horses slept in the stables, and on the roof sat the pigeons fast asleep with their heads under their wings. And when he came into the palace, the flies slept on the walls, and the cook in the kitchen was still holding up her hand as if she would beat the boy, and the maid sat with a black fowl in her hand ready to be plucked.

Then he went on still further and all was so still that he could hear every breath he drew. At last he came to the old tower and opened the door of the little room in which Briar Rose was. There she lay fast asleep and looked so beautiful that he could not take his eyes off her, and he stooped down and gave her a kiss. But the moment he kissed her, she opened her eyes, and smiled upon him.

Then they went out together, and presently the king and queen also awoke, and all the court, and they gazed on each other with great wonder.

And the horses got up and shook themselves, and the dogs jumped about and barked; the pigeons took their heads from under their wings, looked about, and flew into the fields; the flies on the walls buzzed away; the fire in the kitchen blazed up and cooked the dinner, and the roast meat turned round again; the cook gave the boy the box on his ear so that he cried out, and the maid went on plucking the fowl.

And then was the wedding of the prince and Briar Rose celebrated, and they lived happily all their lives long.

—*The Brothers Grimm.*

Why the Bear Has a Stumpy Tail

ONE winter's day the bear met the fox, who came slinking along with a string of fish he had stolen.

"Hi! stop a minute! Where did you get those from?" demanded the bear.

"Oh, my lord Bruin, I've been out fishing and caught them," said the fox.

So the bear had a mind to learn to fish, too, and bade the fox tell him how he was to set about it.

"Oh, it is quite easy," answered the fox, "and soon learned. You've only got to go upon the ice, and cut a hole and stick your tail down through it, and hold it there as long as you can. You're not to mind if it smarts a little; that's when the fish bite. The longer you hold it there, the more fish you'll get; then all at once out with it, with a cross pull sideways and a strong pull, too."

Well, the bear did as the fox said, and though he felt very cold, and his tail smarted very much, he kept it a long, long time down in the hole, till at last it was frozen in, though of course he did not know that. Then he pulled it out with a strong pull, and it snapped short off.

And that's why Bruin goes about with a stumpy tail to this day!

The Doggies' Promenade

THREE dogs went out for a promenade
    All on a summer's day.
There was Mr. Dog and Mrs. Dog,
    And little Doggie Tray.

Old Papa Dog wore a stove-pipe hat
    And a button-hole bouquet,
And a bamboo cane, and a gold watch-chain,
    And a suit of parson gray.

And Mamma Dog had a new silk gown,
    And a bonnet trimmed with blue,
And a high-heeled boot on each dainty foot
    And a brooch and bracelets, too.

Wee Baby Dog had a round Scotch cap,
    And a kilt way down to his knee,
And satin bows all over his clothes,
    And pockets—one, two, three.

And as they walked down the crowded street,
    They were proud as proud could be;
For they were dressed in their very best,
    As everyone could see.

But a mischievous cat on the sidewalk stood.
    No coat, no hat had she.
So she laughed at the dress and the pom-
      pousness
    Of the dog and his family.

Mr. Dog growled deep, and sprang at the cat,
    And chased her up and down
With an angry cry, and a flashing eye,
    Throughout the wondering town.

But he tripped in his haste 'gainst a big
    round stone,
    And fell in the slippery street;
And when he arose, lo! his stylish clothes
    Were mud from head to feet.

And Mrs. Dog when she saw his plight
    With horror swooned away,
And sank right down, with her silken gown,
    On a heap of soft red clay.

Wee Baby Dog was in sad distress:
    He sought for his cap in vain;
His kilt was torn; he was all forlorn,
    And his tears fell down like rain.

But the roguish cat at her fireside sat,
    And thought of her fun that day;
And she jumped and danced, and purred
    and pranced
    At the doggies running away.

The Three Bears

IN A COUNTRY far away there once lived a little girl called Goldilocks because her hair shone like gold.

One day she went into the woods to gather wild flowers and into the fields to chase the butterflies. She ran on and on, taking little heed of the way until she found herself in a lonely spot, and just ahead of her there stood a snug little house. It was the house in which three bears lived, though they were not at home just then.

They were the Big Bear, the Middle-sized Bear, and the Little Bear.

The door was ajar. Goldilocks pushed it wider, and found the room empty. So she boldly walked in. What did she find in the kitchen but three bowls of porridge, just as the three bears had left them to cool. She tasted the largest bowl, which belonged to the Big Bear.

It was too hot.

Then she tasted the middle-sized bowl, which belonged to the Middle-sized Bear.

It was too cold.

Then she tasted the smallest bowl, which belonged to the Little Bear.

It was just right, so she ate every bit of the porridge in that bowl.

She went into the parlor, and there stood three chairs.

She tried the biggest chair, which belonged to the Big Bear.

It was too high.

She tried the middle-sized chair, which belonged to the Middle-sized Bear.

It was too broad.

Then she tried the little chair, which belonged to the Little Bear.

It was just right, and she sat in it so hard that she broke it!

Now by this time Goldilocks was very tired, so she climbed the stairs to the chamber, where she found three beds.

She tried the largest bed, which belonged to the Big Bear.

It was too soft.

She tried the middle-sized bed, which belonged to the Middle-sized Bear.

It was too hard.

Then she tried the smallest bed, which belonged to the Little Bear.

It was just right, so she lay down upon it and soon fell fast asleep.

Now while Goldilocks was sleeping soundly, the three bears came home from their walk in the woods.

They went straight to the kitchen to get their porridge, but when the Big Bear went to his bowl, he growled in his big voice: "Somebody has been tasting my porridge!"

And when the Middle-sized Bear saw her bowl, she said in her middle-sized voice: "Somebody has been tasting my porridge!"

But when the Little Bear saw his bowl, he piped up in his little voice: "Somebody has been tasting my porridge and eaten it every bit!"

Then all three bears went into the parlor, and the Big Bear growled in his big voice: "Somebody has been sitting in my chair!"

And the Middle-sized Bear said in her

A Color Illustration *(over)*

The three bears came home from their
walk in the woods.

middle-sized voice: "Somebody has been sitting in my chair!"

But when the Little Bear saw his chair, he piped up in his little voice: "Somebody has been sitting in my chair and broken it all to pieces!"

So they all three climbed the stairs, and when they went into their chamber, the Big Bear growled in his big voice: "Somebody has been tumbling in my bed!"

And the Middle-sized Bear said in her middle-sized voice: "Somebody has been tumbling in my bed!"

And the Little Bear piped up in his little voice: "Somebody has been tumbling in my bed, and here she is!"

At this Goldilocks awoke in a fright, and jumped out of bed in a twinkling, ran down the stairs, out the door and away just as fast as her legs could carry her, and never, never did she go near the house of the three bears again.

Why Cats Wash after Eating

A LONG time ago cats washed before eating just as people do. This is how it came to be changed:

An old cat who was very hungry caught a mouse and was about to eat it immediately, when the poor mouse began to beg for his life. "O Kitty, please don't eat me! Let me go!" he pleaded.

"No," said the cat, "I will not let you go. I am hungry."

Then the mouse had an idea. "Well, Kitty," he said, "if you must eat me, you must. But aren't you going to wash first? All nice persons wash before eating."

"Yes, that is so," agreed the cat, and began to wash her face.

She forgot to hold the mouse, and away he scampered through a hole in the wall.

"Oh, what a trick!" cried the cat.

She spread the news of her experience to all the other cats, and so ever since that time all cats eat first and then wash their faces.

Have you not seen your cat do it?

The History of Dick Whittington

IN THE reign of famous King Edward III, there was a little boy called Dick Whittington, whose father and mother died when he was very young. As poor Dick was not old enough to work, he was very badly off.

Now Dick had heard many, many very strange things about the great city called London, for the country people at that time thought that folks in London were all fine gentlemen and ladies; that there was singing and music there all day long; and that the streets were all paved with gold.

One day a large wagon and eight horses, all with bells at their heads, drove through the village while Dick was standing by the sign-post. He thought that this wagon must be going to the fine town of London. So he took courage, and asked the wagoner to let him walk with him by the side of the wagon. The wagoner told him he might go if he would, so off they set together.

So Dick got safe to London, and was in such a hurry to see the fine streets paved all over with gold, that he did not even stay to thank the wagoner, but ran off as fast as his legs would carry him, thinking every moment to come upon streets paved with gold.

Poor Dick ran till he was tired, and at last, finding that every way he turned he saw nothing but dirt instead of gold, he sat down in a dark corner and cried himself to sleep.

Little Dick remained there all night, and next morning, being very hungry, he got up and walked about, and asked everybody he met to give him a half-penny to keep him from starving.

At last a good-natured looking gentleman saw how hungry he looked. "Why don't you go to work, my lad?" said he to Dick.

"That I would, but I do not know how to get any," answered Dick.

"If you are willing, come along with me," said the gentleman, and took him to a hay-field, where Dick worked briskly, and lived merrily till the hay was made.

After this he found himself as badly off as before; and being almost starved again, he laid himself down at the door of Mr. Fitzwarren, a rich merchant. Here he was soon seen by the cook-maid, who was an ill-tempered creature, and happened just then to be very busy dressing dinner for her master and mistress; so she called out to poor Dick: "What business have you there, you lazy rogue? If you do not take yourself away, we will see how you will like a sousing of some dish-water; I have some here hot enough to make you jump."

Just at that time Mr. Fitzwarren himself came home to dinner; and when he saw a dirty ragged boy lying at the door, he said to him: "Why do you lie there, my boy? You seem old enough to work; I am afraid you are inclined to be lazy."

"No, indeed, sir," said Dick to him, "that is not the case, for I would work with all my heart, but I do not know anybody, and I believe I am very sick for the want of food."

"Poor fellow, get up; let me see what ails you."

Dick tried to rise but lay down again, being too weak to stand, for he had not eaten any food for three days. So the kind merchant ordered him to be taken into the house, and have a good dinner given him, and be kept to do what work he was able to do for the cook.

Little Dick would have lived very happily in this good family if it had not been for the ill-natured cook. She used to say: "You are under me, so look sharp; clean the spit and the dripping-pan, make the fires, wind up the jack, and do all the scullery work nimbly or—" and she would shake the ladle at him. At last her ill-usage of him was told to Alice, Mr. Fitzwarren's daughter, who told the cook she should be turned away if she did not treat him kinder.

The behavior of the cook was now a little better, but Dick had another hardship to get over. His bed stood in a garret, where there were so many holes in the floor and the walls that every night he was tormented with rats and mice. A gentleman having

given Dick a penny for cleaning his shoes, he bought a cat with it, and hid her in the garret. He always took care to carry a part of his dinner to her; and in a short time he had no more trouble with rats and mice.

Soon after this, his master had a ship ready to sail; and as it was the custom that all his servants should have some chance for good fortune as well as himself, he called them all into the parlor and asked them what they would send out.

They all had something except poor Dick, who had neither money nor goods, and so had not come into the parlor with the rest. Miss Alice guessed what was the matter, and ordered him to be called in. She then said: "I will lay down some money for him from my own purse." But her father told her: "This will not do, for it must be something of his own."

When poor Dick heard this, he said: "I have nothing but a cat which I bought for a penny."

"Fetch your cat then, my lad," said Mr. Fitzwarren, "and let her go."

With tears in his eyes, Dick brought down poor puss and gave her to the captain.

All the company laughed at Dick's odd venture; and Miss Alice, who felt pity for him, gave him some money to buy another cat.

This, and many other marks of kindness shown him by Miss Alice, made the ill-tempered cook jealous of poor Dick, and she began to use him more cruelly than ever, and always made game of him for sending his cat to sea.

At last Dick could not bear it any longer, and he thought he would run away from his

place; so he packed up his few things, and started very early in the morning, on Allhallows Day, the first of November. He walked as far as Halloway, and there sat down on a stone, which to this day is called "Whittington's Stone," and began to think which road he should take.

While he was thinking what he should do, the Bells of Bow Church, which at that time were only six, began to ring, and at their sound seemed to say to him:

"Turn again, Whittington,
Thrice Lord Mayor of London."

"Lord Mayor of London!" said he to himself. "Why, to be sure, I would put up with almost anything now, to be Lord Mayor of London and ride in a fine coach when I grow to be a man! Well, I will go back, and think nothing of the scolding of the old cook, if I am to be Lord Mayor of London at last."

Dick went back, and was lucky enough to get into the house, and set about his work before the old cook came downstairs.

We must now follow Mistress Puss to the coast of Africa. The ship with the cat on board was a long time at sea; and was at last driven by the winds on a part of the coast of Barbary, where the only people were the Moors, unknown to the English. The people came in great numbers to see the sailors, because they were of different color to themselves, and treated them civilly; and, when they became better acquainted, were very eager to buy the fine things that the ship was loaded with.

When the captain saw this, he sent patterns of the best things he had to the king of the country; who was so much pleased with them that he sent for the captain to come to the palace. Here they were placed, as it is the custom of the country, on rich carpets flowered with gold and silver. The king and queen were seated at the upper end of the room; and a number of dishes were brought in for dinner. They had not sat long, when a vast number of rats and mice rushed in, and devoured all the meat in an instant. The captain wondered at this, and asked if these vermin were not unpleasant.

"Oh, yes," said they, "very offensive; and the king would give half his treasure to be freed of them, for they not only destroy his dinner, as you see, but they assault him in his chamber, and even in bed, so that he is obliged to be watched while he is sleeping, for fear of them."

The captain remembered poor Whittington and his cat, and told the king he had a creature on board the ship that would despatch all these vermin immediately. The king jumped so high at the joy which the news gave him, that his turban dropped off his head. "Bring this creature to me," said he; "and if she will perform what you say, I will load your ship with gold and jewels in exchange for her."

Away went the captain to the ship, while another dinner was got ready. He put Puss under his arm, and arrived at the place just in time to see the table full of rats. When the cat saw them, she did not wait for bidding, but jumped out of the captain's arms, and in a few minutes laid almost all the rats and mice dead at her feet. The rest of them in their fright scampered away to their holes.

The king, having seen the exploits of Mistress Puss, and being informed that her kittens would stock the whole country, and keep it free from rats, bargained with the captain for the whole ship's cargo, and then gave him ten times as much for the cat as for all the rest.

The captain then took leave of the royal party, and set sail with a fair wind for England, and after a happy voyage arrived safe in London.

Early one morning Mr. Fitzwarren had just come to his counting-house when somebody came tap, tap, at the door.

"Who's there?" asked Mr. Fitzwarren.

"A friend," answered the other. "I come to bring you good news of your ship *Unicorn.*"

The merchant opened the door, and whom should he see waiting but the captain with a cabinet of jewels. He then told the story of the cat, and showed the rich present

that the king and queen had sent to poor Dick. As soon as the merchant heard this, he called out to his servants:

"Go send him in, and tell him of his fame;
Pray call him Mr. Whittington by name."

Mr. Fitzwarren now showed himself to be a good man; for when some of his servants said so great a treasure was too much for Dick, he answered: "God forbid I should deprive him of the value of a single penny! It is his own, and he shall have it to a farthing."

He then sent for Dick, who at that time was scouring pots for the cook, and was quite dirty. He tried to excuse himself from coming into the counting-house, saying, "The room is swept, and my shoes are dirty and full of hobnails." But the merchant

39

ordered him to come in, and had a chair set for him. So Dick began to think they were making game of him, and said to them: "Do not play tricks with a poor simple boy, but let me go down again, if you please, to my work."

"Indeed, Mr. Whittington," said the merchant, "we are all quite in earnest with you, and I most heartily rejoice in the news that these gentlemen have brought you; for the captain has sold your cat to the King of Barbary, and brought you in return for her more riches than I possess in the whole world; and I wish you may long enjoy them!"

Mr. Fitzwarren then told the men to open the great treasure they had brought with them, and said: "Mr. Whittington has nothing to do but to put it in some place of safety."

Poor Dick hardly knew how to behave himself for joy. He begged his master to take what part of the riches he pleased, since he owed it all to his kindness.

"No, no," answered Mr. Fitzwarren, "this is all your own; and I have no doubt but you will use it well."

Dick next asked his mistress, and then Miss Alice, to accept a part of his good fortune; but they would not, and at the same time told him they felt great joy at his good success. But this poor fellow was too kind-hearted to keep it all to himself; so he made a present to the captain, the mate, and the rest of Mr. Fitzwarren's servants, and even to the ill-natured old cook.

After this Mr. Fitzwarren advised him to send for a proper tailor, and get himself dressed like a gentleman; and told him he was welcome to live in his house till he could provide himself with a better.

When Whittington's face was washed, his hair curled, his hat cocked, and he was dressed in a nice suit of clothes, he was as handsome and genteel as any young man who visited at Mr. Fitzwarren's. Miss Alice, who had once been so kind to him and thought of him with pity, now looked upon him as fit to be her sweetheart; and the more so, no doubt, because Whittington was now always thinking what he could do to oblige her, and making her the prettiest presents that could be.

Mr. Fitzwarren soon saw their love for each other, and proposed to join them in marriage; and to this they both readily agreed. A day for the wedding was soon fixed; and they were attended to church by the Lord Mayor, the court of aldermen, the sheriffs, and a great number of the richest merchants in London, whom they afterwards treated with a very rich feast.

History tells us that Mr. Whittington and his lady lived in great splendor, had several children and were very happy. He was Sheriff of London, thrice Lord Mayor, and received the honor of knighthood by Henry V. He entertained this king and his queen at dinner, after his conquest of France, so grandly that the king said: "Never had prince such a subject." And when Sir Richard heard this, he said: "Never had subject such a prince."

Three Billy Goats Gruff

ONCE upon a time there were three Billy Goats who went up the hillside to make themselves fat.

The name of all three was "Gruff."

On the way up there was a bridge over a brook. And under that bridge there lived a great ugly Troll. His eyes were as big as saucers, and his nose was as long as your arm.

First of all came the youngest Billy Goat Gruff to cross the bridge.

Trip Trap! went the bridge as he passed over.

"Who's that tripping over my bridge?" roared the Troll.

"Oh, it is only I, the tiniest Billy Goat Gruff, and I am going up the hillside to make myself fat," said the Billy Goat in such a very small voice.

"Ho, I am coming to gobble you up!" said the Troll.

"Oh, no, pray do not take me! I am too little," said the Billy Goat. "Wait a bit until the next Billy Goat Gruff comes. He's much bigger!"

"Well, be off with you!" said the Troll.

A little while after came the second Billy Goat Gruff to cross the bridge.

Trip Trap! Trip Trap! went the bridge.

"Who's that tripping over my bridge?" roared the Troll.

"Oh, it is only I, the second Billy Goat Gruff, and I am going up the hillside to make myself fat," said the Billy Goat, who hadn't such a very small voice.

"Ho, I am coming to gobble you up!" said the Troll.

"Oh, no, pray do not take me! Wait a bit until the big Billy Goat comes. He's much bigger."

"Very well. Be off with you!" said the Troll.

But just then came the big Billy Goat Gruff.

Trip Trap! Trip Trap! Trip Trap! went the bridge, for this Billy Goat was so heavy the bridge cracked under him.

"Who's that tripping over my bridge?" roared the Troll.

"It is I, the big Billy Goat Gruff!" said the Billy Goat, who had a big hoarse voice.

"Ho, now I am coming to gobble you up!" roared the Troll.

"Well, come along! I've got two spears,
And I'll poke your eyeballs out at your
      ears;
I've got besides two curling-stones,
And I'll crush you to bits, body and
      bones."

That was what the big Billy Goat said. He flew at the Troll, poked his eyes out with his horns, crushed him to bits, body and bones, and tossed him into the brook. After that he went on up the hillside.

There the three Billy Goats grew so fat they were scarce able to walk home again; and if the fat hasn't fallen off them, why, they're fat still; and so—

Snip, snap, snout,
This tale's told out.

The Greatest of All

IN FAR-AWAY Japan there once lived a rat and his wife, whose only daughter was very beautiful. They were proud of her and dreamed, as parents will, of a grand marriage. A young rat of noble family came to woo her, and the father thought he could have no better son-in-law, for he was proud of his rodent blood. But the mother was like many people who think they are made of special clay; she had a poor opinion of others of her own race, and would not listen to the proposal. "When one has a daughter of the highest charm," she said, "one may well expect a son-in-law equally high."

"Go to the sun at once, then," cried the impatient father. "There is nothing above him."

"I was thinking of that," answered his wife, "and now that you suggest it, we will call there tomorrow."

So the next morning the proud father and the haughty mother took their daughter to the sun.

"Lord Sun," said the mother, "let me present our only daughter, who is so beautiful that there is nothing like her in the world. Naturally we desire a son-in-law as wonderful as she is and we have come to you first of all."

"I am extremely flattered by your proposal," said the sun, "but you do me too much honor. There is someone greater than I; it is the cloud. Look, if you do not believe." ... And at that moment the cloud arrived and with one waft of his folds shut out the sun with all his golden rays.

"Very well; let us speak to the cloud, then," said the mother, not in the least put out.

"Immensely honored, I am sure," replied the cloud in his turn, "but you are again mistaken. There is someone greater than I; it is the wind. You shall see." . . . And at that moment along came the wind, and with one blow swept the cloud out of sight. Then he overturned the father, mother, and daughter, and tumbled with them pell-mell, at the foot of an old wall.

"Quick, quick," cried the mother, struggling to her feet, "let us repeat our compliments to the wind."

"You'd better address yourself to the wall," growled the wind roughly. "You see very well he is greater than I, for he stops me and makes me draw back."

No sooner had she heard these words than the mother faced about and offered her daughter to the wall.

But now the daughter drew back. To please her mother, she had given up the young rat who had wooed her, and had consented to marry the sun, in spite of his blinding rays, or the cloud, in spite of his sulky look, or even the wind, in spite of his brusque manner; but an old, broken wall! No, never!

Fortunately the wall also excused himself. "Certainly," he said, "I can stop the wind, who can sweep away the cloud, who can cover up the sun. But there is someone greater than I; it is the rat. He can pass through my body, and can even reduce me to powder with his teeth, if he chooses. Believe me, you need seek no better son-in-law; there is nothing in the world greater than the rat."

"Do you hear that, wife; do you hear that?" cried the father in triumph. "Didn't I always say so?"

"Quite true! you always did," returned the mother in wonder, and suddenly she glowed with pride in her ancient name and race.

So they all three went home, very happy and contented, and on the morrow the lovely daughter was married to her faithful rat lover.

—*Adapted from the Japanese.*

The Little Red Hen

THE Little Red Hen lived in a barnyard where there was also a Cat, a Rat, and a Pig. The Cat usually lay napping lazily in the barn door, not even bothering to scare away the Rat who ran about. As for the Pig in the sty—he did not care what happened so long as he had all he could eat. But the Little Red Hen spent most of her time scratching for worms for herself and her chicks. A very busy Red Hen she was!

One day as she went about in her pickety-peckety fashion, she found a seed. Carrying it about the barnyard, she asked one and then another what it was until the Rat said it was a grain of wheat, and if it was planted it would grow, and when ripe could be made into flour and then into bread.

The Little Red Hen thought of the Pig,

upon whom time must hang heavily, and of the Cat with nothing to do, and of the great fat Rat with his idle hours, and she called out loudly, "Who will plant this grain of wheat?"

"Not I," said the Cat.

"Not I," said the Rat.

"Not I," said the Pig.

"Then I will," said the Little Red Hen, and she did.

All summer long the Little Red Hen scratched for worms to feed her chicks, while the Pig grew fat, and the Cat grew fat, and the Rat grew fat, and the wheat grew tall and ready for the harvest.

When the Little Red Hen saw the wheat was ready to be cut, she ran about, calling briskly, "Who will cut the wheat?"

"Not I," said the Cat.

"Not I," said the Rat.

"Not I," said the Pig.

"Then I will," said the Little Red Hen, and she did.

There on the ground lay the wheat nicely cut and ready to be threshed. The Little Red Hen looked about hopefully and asked, "Who will thresh this wheat?"

"Not I," said the Cat.

"Not I," said the Rat.

"Not I," said the Pig.

"Well, then I will," said the Little Red Hen, and she did.

When the wheat was all threshed and ready to be ground into flour, the Little Red Hen looked about again, and asked, "Who will take this wheat to the mill for grinding?"

A Color Illustration *(over)*

"Then I will," said the Little Red Hen.
And soon the bread was made.

"Not I," said the Cat.

"Not I," said the Rat.

"Not I," said the Pig.

"Then I will," said the Little Red Hen, and she did.

When the wheat was ground into flour and was ready for bread, the Little Red Hen took it home. By this time the Little Red Hen was rather discouraged, but once more she looked about at the others and asked, "Who will make this wheat into bread?"

"Not I," said the Cat.

"Not I," said the Rat.

"Not I," said the Pig.

"Then I will," said the Little Red Hen, and she did.

Soon the bread was made and in the oven. A delicious odor was wafted on the autumn breeze. When the bread was baked, the Little Red Hen took it out of the oven. Then, probably because she had acquired the habit, she looked about and called out, "Who will eat this bread?"

"I will," cried the Cat.

"I will," cried the Rat.

"I will," cried the Pig.

"No, you won't," said the Little Red Hen. "I will," and she did.

The Fox and the Stork

ONE day the fox thought he would play a joke on his friend the stork. He stopped at her house and said, "You must dine with me today, for I have had luck, and the soup will be rich."

So the stork went. But when they went in to dine, the stork found that the dish in which the soup was served was so flat that she could only dip in the point of her bill while the fox could lap it up with his tongue. "It grieves me," said the fox, "to see you make so poor a meal. I fear it is not to your mind."

The stork did not complain, but at the end of the meal told her host that it was now his turn to come and dine with her.

So the next day, true to the hour, the fox came. "Good-day," said the stork. "Now I hope you will feel you are quite at home."

The smell of the stew was fine. But when they sat down to dinner, it was put in a jar with a thin neck, down which the stork thrust her long bill with ease. But all the fox could do was to lick the rim of it.

When it came time for the fox to leave, he made his bow with bad grace, but the stork only smiled and said, "Tit for tat. Good cat, good rat."

—*Aesop.*

The Traveling Musicians

A FARMER once had a donkey that had been a faithful servant to him a great many years, but who was now growing too old to work. His master therefore was tired of keeping him and began to think of putting an end to him. But the donkey saw that some mischief was in the wind, and took himself slyly off, and began his journey towards the city, "for there," thought he, "I may turn musician."

After he had travelled a little way, he spied a dog lying by the roadside and panting as if he were very tired.

"What makes you pant so, my friend?" said the donkey.

"Alas!" said the dog, "my master was going to kill me because I am old and weak, and can no longer make myself useful to him in hunting; so I ran away. But what can I do to earn my livelihood?"

"I am going to the great city to turn musician. Suppose you go with me, and try what you can do in the same way."

The dog said he was willing, and they jogged on together.

They had not gone far before they saw a cat sitting in the middle of the road and making a most rueful face.

"Pray, my good lady," said the donkey, "what's the matter with you? You look quite out of spirits!"

"Ah me!" said the cat, "how can one be in good spirits when one's life is in danger? Because I am beginning to grow old, and had rather lie at my ease by the fire than run about the house after the mice, my mistress laid hold of me, and was going to drown me. And though I have been lucky enough to get away from her, I do not know what I am to live upon."

"Oh!" said the donkey, "by all means go with us to the great city. You are a good night singer, and may make your fortune as a musician."

The cat was pleased with the thought, and joined the party. Soon afterwards, as they were passing by a farmyard, they saw a cock perched upon a gate and screaming out with all his might and main.

"Bravo!" said the donkey. "Upon my word, you make a famous noise; pray what is all this about?"

"Why," said the cock, "I was just now saying that we should have fine weather for our washing-day, and yet my mistress and the cook don't thank me for my pains, but threaten to cut off my head tomorrow, and make broth of me for the guests that are coming on Sunday!"

"Heaven forbid it!" said the donkey. "Come with us, Master Chanticleer; it will be better, at any rate, than staying here to have your head cut off! Besides, who knows? If we take care to sing in tune, we may get up some kind of a concert: so come along with us."

"With all my heart," said the cock: so they all four went on jollily together.

They could not, however, reach the great city the first day; so when night came on they went into a wood to sleep. The donkey and the dog laid themselves down

under a great tree, and the cat climbed up into the branches; while the cock, thinking that the higher he sat, the safer he should be, flew up to the very top of the tree, and then, according to his custom, before he went to sleep looked out on all sides to see that everything was well. In doing this, he saw afar off something bright and shining; and calling to his companions, he said, "There must be a house no great way off, for I see a light."

"If that be the case," said the donkey, "we had better change our quarters, for our lodging is not the best in the world!"

"Besides," added the dog, "I should not be the worse for a bone or two, or a bit of meat."

So they walked off together towards the spot where Chanticleer had seen the light. As they drew near, it became larger and brighter, till at last they came close to a house in which a gang of robbers lived.

The donkey, being the tallest of the company, marched up to the window and peeped in.

"Well, Donkey," said Chanticleer, "what do you see?"

"What do I see?" replied the donkey. "Why, I see a table spread with all kinds of good things, and robbers sitting round it making merry."

"That would be a noble lodging for us," said the cock.

"Yes," said the donkey, "if we could only get in."

So they consulted together how they should contrive to get the robbers out: and at last they hit upon a plan. The donkey placed himself upright on his hind legs, with his forefeet resting against the window; the dog got upon his back; the cat scrambled up to the dog's shoulders, and the cock flew up and sat upon the cat's head. When all was ready, a signal was given, and they began their music. The donkey brayed, the dog barked, the cat mewed, and the cock crowed; and then they all broke through the window

47

at once, and came tumbling into the room, amongst the broken glass, with a most hideous clatter. The robbers, who had been not a little frightened by the opening concert, had now no doubt that some frightful hobgoblin had broken in upon them, and scampered away as fast as they could.

The coast once clear, our travelers sat down, and ate the meal the robbers had left. Then they put out the lights, and each once more sought out a resting-place to his own liking. The donkey lay down upon a heap of straw in the yard; the dog stretched out upon a mat behind the door; the cat rolled up on the hearth before the warm ashes; and the cock perched upon a beam on the top of the house: and, as they were all rather tired with their journey, they soon fell asleep.

When the robbers saw from afar that the lights were out and that all seemed quiet, they began to think that they had been in too great a hurry to run away; and one of them, who was bolder than the rest, went to see what was going on.

Finding everything still, he marched into the kitchen, and groped about till he found a match. Then, espying the fiery eyes of the cat, he mistook them for live coals, and held the match to them to light it. But the cat sprung at his face and spit and scratched at him. This frightened him dreadfully, and away he ran to the back door. But there the dog jumped up and bit him in the leg; and as he was crossing the yard, the donkey kicked him; and the cock, who had been awakened by the noise, crowed with all his might.

The robber ran back as fast as he could to his comrades, and told the captain "how a horrid witch had got into the house, and had spit at him and scratched his face with her long bony fingers; how a man with a knife in his hand had hidden himself behind the door, and stabbed him in the leg; how a black monster stood in the yard and struck him with a club, and how the devil sat upon the top of the house and cried out, 'Throw the rascal up here!'"

After this the robbers never dared to go back to the house; but the musicians were so pleased with their quarters, that they took up their abode there; and there they are, I dare say, at this very day.

—*The Brothers Grimm.*

48

The Timid Little Rabbit

ONCE upon a time a timid little rabbit lay sleeping beneath a tree. It was the season when nuts were ripening and one of them fell to the ground.

The timid little rabbit awoke with a start.

"Oh!" he cried, "the earth is falling in!"

Without waiting to investigate, off he ran.

By and by he met a squirrel.

"Squirrel, squirrel!" he cried, "the earth is falling in!"

The squirrel was greatly frightened and off he ran with the timid little rabbit.

Soon the two met a fox.

"Fox, fox!" cried the squirrel, "the earth is falling in!"

And off ran the fox with the squirrel and the timid little rabbit.

The three met a tiger.

"Tiger, tiger!" cried the fox, "the earth is falling in!"

And off ran the tiger with the fox, the squirrel, and the timid little rabbit.

The four met a lion.

"Lion, lion!" cried the tiger, "the earth is falling in!"

The lion was not at all frightened. "Who told you?" he asked the tiger.

"Fox told me," said the tiger.

"Squirrel told me," said the fox.

"Rabbit told me," said the squirrel.

"Who told you?" the lion asked the rabbit.

"I was asleep under a tree and when I awoke I heard the earth falling in. I ran away as fast as I could."

"Then," said the lion, "we will go back to that tree where the earth began falling in and see what is the matter."

So the lion took the timid little rabbit on his back and away they went together.

But the others were too frightened to go back and ran on and on, crying to all the animals that they met, "The earth is falling in!"

Soon all the animals were running and calling to each other, "The earth is falling in! The earth is falling in!"

When the lion came to the tree, the rabbit on his back said, "This is the place."

The lion looked about and saw the nut in the leaves.

"Why, little rabbit, the earth is not falling in. You only heard this nut falling on the leaves."

Off rushed the little rabbit, calling joyously to all the animals, "The earth is not falling in!"

The other animals stopped running and began telling each other, "Why, the earth is not falling in!"

But if it had not been for the wise old lion, they might have been running yet.

—An East Indian Story.

The Elves
and the Shoemaker

ONCE upon a time there lived a shoemaker who grew so poor, though through no fault of his own, that he had leather enough to make only one pair of shoes.

That evening he cut out the shoes, intending to put them together the next morning, and then because he had a clear conscience, he said his prayers, lay down quietly in his bed and soon was asleep.

In the morning he was ready to sit down to his toil before he noticed that the pair of shoes stood on his table all finished and ready to sell. He was so astonished at the sight that he had no words to express his surprise. He took up the shoes, turned them over and over—they were so skilfully made he could not find a stitch out of place.

A customer soon came and gladly paid more than the usual price. The shoemaker lost no time to buy leather for two pairs of shoes. That evening he cut them out and next morning found the two pairs of shoes all finished standing on his table.

Soon two customers stepped in, paying him so well he bought leather for four pairs of shoes. The morning after, he found the four pairs finished and standing on his table. So it went. What he cut out in the evening was finished next morning, and soon he was in comfortable circumstances again.

Just before Christmas the shoemaker said to his wife, "What do you think of our staying up tonight and discovering who lends us the helping hand?"

His wife agreed, and at midnight some naked little men came into the shop and stitched and sewed and hammered. Before dawn all the shoes were made and then the little men ran away.

The next day the shoemaker's wife said, "We must show the little men we are grateful. They wore no clothes and must be very cold. I'll make them each a coat, vest and trousers, a shirt apiece, and knit each a pair of stockings, and you shall make them each a pair of shoes."

And on Christmas eve how astonished the little men were to find all the garments laid out for them!

They put on the clothes with haste and skipped about the room, singing:

"Now we are boys too fine to see,
Why should we longer cobblers be?"

At last they danced out at the door. And that is the last anyone has seen of the little men, though the shoemaker prospered as long as he lived.

—*The Brothers Grimm.*

Jack and the Beanstalk

ONCE upon a time a poor widow had an only son Jack and a cow named Milky White. All the two had to live on was her milk, which they sold at market.

But one morning Milky-White gave no milk.

"What shall we do?" wailed the widow. "We must sell Milky-White and with the money start a shop or something."

"All right," agreed Jack. "I'll soon sell her and then we'll see what we can do," and off he led her by the halter.

He hadn't gone far when he met a funny-looking man who said to him, "Good-morning, Jack. Where are you off to?"

"To market, to sell our cow," answered Jack.

"I wonder if you know how many beans make five," said the man, giving Jack a keen look and thrusting his hands into his pockets.

"Two in each hand and one in your mouth," said Jack, sharp as a needle.

"Right you are! And here are the very beans themselves!" the man replied and pulled some strange-looking beans out of his pocket. "Your cow for these beans," he offered.

"Go along!" said Jack.

"Ah, you don't know what these beans are! If you plant them overnight, by morning they grow right up to the sky," exclaimed the funny-looking man.

"Really?" said Jack, and he handed over Milky-White's halter and pocketed the beans.

By the time he got home, it was dusk and his mother met him at the door, saying, "Oh, you sold Milky-White! How much did you get?"

"You'll never guess. See, these magical beans!"

"What!" exclaimed she. "You've given away our Milky-White for a few paltry beans? Here they go out the window! To bed with you without a sup to drink or a bite to eat this night!"

So Jack climbed to his little attic room, sad and sorry for his mother's sake as well as for the loss of his supper.

When he woke, the sun was shining into part of his room, but all the rest of it was quite dark. Jack jumped up, dressed and went to the window. And what do you think he saw? Why, a big beanstalk which went right up to the sky; the man had spoken the truth after all!

The beanstalk grew so close to Jack's window, all he had to do was give a jump and he was on it. It was just like a big ladder.

Jack climbed and climbed and climbed. At last he reached the sky, and there he found a long, wide road. He walked and walked and walked till he came to a great tall house, and on the bench at the door sat a great tall woman.

"Good-morning," said Jack politely. "Could you give me some breakfast?"

"It's breakfast you'll be if you don't move off from here!" replied the great tall woman. "My husband's an ogre and likes boys broiled on toast. He'll soon be coming."

"Oh please, ma'am, I've had nothing to eat since yesterday morning. I may as well be broiled as die of hunger," Jack pleaded.

Well, the ogre's wife took Jack into the kitchen and gave him bread and cheese and a huge mug of milk.

Jack hadn't half finished when Thump! Thump! Thump! the whole house shook with someone's coming.

"Good gracious! It's my old man. Jump in here," and the ogre's wife bundled Jack into the oven.

The ogre came in. He was a big one, to be sure. At his belt he had three calves strung up by the heels.

Unhooking them and throwing them on the table, he said, "Wife, broil a couple of these for my breakfast. Ha! what's this I smell?

"Fee-Fi-Fo-Fum,
I smell the blood of an Englishman!
Be he alive, or be he dead,
I'll have his bones to grind my bread."

"Nonsense, dear! Perhaps you smell the scraps of the little boy you enjoyed at yesterday's dinner! Now go wash, and I'll have your breakfast ready when you come back."

So off he went, and Jack peeped out of the oven, but the woman said, "Wait till after breakfast! He always dozes then."

Well, after breakfast the ogre went to a big chest, lifted out some great bags of gold and counted the money till his head began to nod.

He snored till the whole house shook. Then Jack tiptoed by him, took one of the bags and peltered off to the beanstalk. He climbed down and down and down till he got home. He and his mother lived on the gold till they came to the end of it.

Then one fine morning Jack climbed up the beanstalk till at last he came out on the road that took him to the great tall house. And there on the door step was the great tall woman.

"Good-morning," said Jack. "Could you give me something to eat?"

"Aren't you the boy who was here once before?" she asked. "Do you know on that very day the ogre missed one bag of gold?"

"I am so hungry I can't speak, or I dare

say I could tell you something about that," said Jack.

So, to hear his story, she took him in, but he had scarcely begun to eat when Thump! Thump! Thump! they heard the ogre's footsteps.

The wife hid Jack in the oven, and all happened as before. In came the ogre, who said, "Fee-Fi-Fo-Fum," and breakfasted on three broiled oxen. Then he said, "Wife, bring me the hen that lays the golden eggs," and when she brought it, he said, "Lay!" and the hen laid an egg all of gold.

Then the ogre began to nod, and he snored till the house shook. Jack crept out of the oven on tiptoe, caught up the golden hen and was off.

But this time the hen cackled, which woke the ogre. Just as Jack got out of the house, he heard him shout, "Wife! Wife! What have you done with my golden hen?"

But that was all Jack heard, for with a leap and a bound he reached the beanstalk and hurried down and down and down.

And when he reached home, he showed the wonderful hen to his mother, who was astonished to see that it laid a golden egg every time Jack said, "Lay!" And with what the eggs brought, they lived in comfort.

Well, Jack was not long content, so one fine morning he went to the beanstalk, and he climbed and climbed and climbed till he reached the top. But this time when he came near the ogre's house, he hid behind a bush till he saw the great tall woman come out to get a pail of water.

Then he crept into the house and climbed into the copper. He hadn't been there long when he heard Thump! Thump!

Thump! and in came both the ogre and his wife. The ogre sniffed and said,

"Fee-Fi-Fo-Fum,
I smell the blood of an Englishman!"

"Do you, dearie?" asked the ogre's wife, and then she added quickly, "If it's that little rogue who stole your gold and your hen, we'll find him in the oven," and they both rushed over to it.

Luckily Jack wasn't there, and the ogre's wife said, "Why, of course you smell the boy I've just broiled for your breakfast. It's queer you don't know the difference between live and dead after all these years!"

So the ogre sat down to breakfast, but every now and then he'd get up to search the cupboards and everything. But he didn't think of the copper. When he had finished eating, he called, "Wife, wife, bring me my golden harp."

When she put it on the table before him, he said, "Sing!" and the harp sang beautifully till the ogre fell asleep and snored like thunder.

Then Jack crept out of the copper and over to the table, crawled up and seized the harp and dashed to the door. But the harp called out loudly, "Master! Master!" and the ogre woke up just in time to see Jack running off with the harp.

Jack ran as fast as ever he could, the ogre after him. Down the beanstalk Jack plunged. The ogre hesitated a bit before he trusted himself to such a ladder, then followed. Jack climbed down and down and down, and when near the bottom he shouted, "Mother, bring the axe!"

His mother came rushing out with the axe, but when she came to the beanstalk, she stood stockstill with fright, for she saw the ogre climbing down after Jack. Jack jumped down, took the axe, and gave one chop at the beanstalk, which cut it half in two. The ogre felt the beanstalk shake and quiver, so he stopped to see what was the matter. Then Jack gave another chop, and the beanstalk toppled over. Down fell the ogre and broke his crown.

Then Jack showed his mother his golden harp, and what with showing that and selling the golden eggs, Jack and his mother grew rich and the two lived happily ever after.

—*From the English.*

The Tortoise Who Would Talk

ONCE upon a time a tortoise was living in a pond in the Himalaya Mountains. He loved to talk and was forever chatting with all the animals and birds who came to the pond. Among them were two young wild ducks who stopped there to feed for the summer. The tortoise talked to them and at length the three became good friends.

When it came time for the ducks to leave for their winter home, they said, "Friend Tortoise, the place where we are going, the Golden Cave on Mount Beautiful, is a delightful spot. Will you come with us?"

"But how can I get there?" asked the Tortoise.

"We can take you if you can only hold your tongue. You will have to keep your mouth closed and say nothing to anybody."

"Oh! that I can do easily."

So the ducks brought a stick. They made the tortoise take hold of the middle of the stick, and they themselves took the two ends in their mouths. Then they flew up in the air and winged their way toward Mount Beautiful.

As they flew thus over the farms and villages, the people ran out in surprise. "See!" they cried. "Two wild ducks are carrying a tortoise along on a stick. Isn't that funny?"

The wind brought their words up to the tortoise, and he thought, "If my friends choose to carry me, what is that to you, you wretched slaves?"

But alas! No sooner had the thought flashed through his mind than he opened his mouth to utter the words.

Down, down he fell to the ground and split in two—the poor tortoise who *would* talk.

—*A Story from India.*

Wee Robin's Christmas Song

THERE was an old gray pussy, and she went away down by a waterside, and there she saw a robin redbreast hopping on a brier bush. And pussy said, "Where are you going, Wee Robin?"

And Wee Robin said, "I'm going away to the king to sing him a song this good Christmas morning."

And pussy said, "Come here, Wee Robin, and I'll let you see a bonnie white ring around my neck."

But Wee Robin said, "No, no! gray pussy, no, no! You worried the wee mouse, but you will not worry me."

So Wee Robin flew away till he came to a garden wall, and there he saw a gray greedy hawk sitting. And gray greedy hawk said, "Where are you going, Wee Robin?"

And Wee Robin said, "I'm going away to the king to sing him a song this good Christmas morning."

And gray greedy hawk said, "Come here, Wee Robin, and I'll let you see a bonnie feather in my wing."

But Wee Robin said, "No, no! gray greedy hawk, no, no! You pecked all the wee birds, but you will not peck me!"

So Wee Robin flew away till he came to a hollow on the mountain side, and there he saw a sly fox sitting. And sly fox said, "Where are you going, Wee Robin?"

And Wee Robin said, "I'm going away to the king to sing him a song this good Christmas morning."

And sly fox said, "Come here, Wee Robin, and I'll let you see a bonnie spot on the tip of my tail."

But Wee Robin said, "No, no! sly fox, no, no! You worried the wee lamb, but you will not worry me."

So Wee Robin flew away till he came to a hillside, and there he saw a rosy-cheeked lad sitting. And the lad said, "Where are you going, Wee Robin?"

And Wee Robin said, "I'm going away to the king to sing him a song this good Christmas morning."

And the rosy-cheeked lad said, "Come here, Wee Robin, and I'll give you some crumbs out of my pocket."

But Wee Robin said, "No, no! rosy-cheeked lad, no, no! You caught the goldfinch, but you will not catch me."

So Wee Robin flew away till he came to the king, and there he sat on a lattice by the king's window and sang the king a bonnie song.

And the king said to the queen, "What shall we give to Wee Robin for singing us this bonnie song?"

And the queen said to the king, "I think we will give him the wee wren to be his wife."

So Wee Robin and the wee wren were married on that good Christmas morning, and the king, and the queen, and all the court danced at the wedding.

After that Wee Robin flew away home to his own waterside and hopped on a brier bush.

—A Scotch Tale.

I Saw a Ship a-Sailing

I SAW a ship a-sailing,
    A-sailing on the sea;
And it was full of pretty things
    For baby and for me.

There were comfits in the cabin,
    And apples in the hold;
The sails were all of velvet,
    And the masts of beaten gold.

The four-and-twenty sailors
    That stood between the decks,
Were four-and-twenty white mice,
    With chains about their necks.

The captain was a duck,
    With a packet on his back;
And when the ship began to move,
    The captain said, "Quack! Quack!"

Puss in Boots

THERE was once a miller who had three sons, and when he died, his estate was divided among them without the help of an attorney, for his fee would have brought the little fortune to nothing. The eldest had the mill, the second the ass, and the youngest had nothing but the cat. He complained that poor indeed was his lot, saying:

"My brothers may get their living easily enough by joining their stocks together. But for me, when I have eaten my cat and made me a fur cap of his skin, I may soon die of hunger and want."

The cat, who had heard all this as he sat listening just inside the door of a cupboard, came out and said gravely: "Do not thus afflict yourself, my good master. You have only to give me a bag and have made for me a pair of boots so I may scamper through the dirt and brambles, and you shall see that your portion is not so bad as you now imagine it to be."

The cat's master had often seen him play many a cunning trick such as hanging by the heels to catch rats and mice, and hiding himself in the meal to make believe he was dead, so while he did not now count very much upon what the cat said, still he did not altogether despair of the cat being able to help him.

He therefore obtained both bag and boots and watched the cat pull on the boots and put the bag around his neck, holding the strings with his forepaws. Bidding his master be of good courage, Puss in Boots sallied forth.

He went straight into a warren in which there were a great number of rabbits. He put some bran and some parsley into his bag and then having stretched out at full length as if dead, waited for some innocent young rabbits to feast on the dainties. Scarcely had he lain down until a foolish young rabbit jumped into his bag, and Puss in Boots quickly drew the strings and killed him without pity.

Puss in Boots was very proud of his prey and hurried with it to the palace and asked to speak to the king. Shown into the apartment of His Majesty, Puss made a low bow and said: "I have brought to you, sir, a rabbit from the warren of my noble lord, the Marquis of Carabas (the title Puss gave to his master), which he commanded me to present to Your Majesty from him."

The king was much pleased, and said, "Tell thy lord Marquis of Carabas I accept his present with pleasure and send my grateful acknowledgment."

Soon afterwards Puss in Boots hid himself among some standing corn. He held his bag open and two fine partridges ran into it. Again he drew the strings quickly and killed them both.

He went to the palace and the king received the partridges as he had the rabbit, and ordered his servants to give Puss something to drink.

In this manner the cat continued to carry presents of game to the king from the Marquis of Carabas at least once a week for two or three months.

One day Puss, having learned the king intended to ride by the river with his daughter, the loveliest princess in all the world, said to his master: "If you will only follow my advice, your fortune is made. Go to the river and bathe just where I show you. Leave the rest to me."

The Marquis of Carabas did exactly as the cat advised, though unable to guess what the cat intended. While he was bathing, the king passed by, and Puss in Boots began to cry out, "Help! Help! My lord Marquis of Carabas is going to be drowned!"

Hearing the cries, the king put his head out of the window of his coach and finding it was the cat who had so often brought him such good game, he ordered his attendants to go quickly to the rescue of my lord Marquis of Carabas. While the servants were drawing the poor Marquis out of the river, Puss in Boots came up to the king's coach and told His Majesty that as his master was bathing, some thieves went off with his clothes as they lay by the riverside, though the truth was that the cunning Puss himself had hidden them under a large stone.

At this news the king commanded the officers of his wardrobe to run and fetch one of his best suits and present it to the Marquis.

After the Marquis was dressed and seated in the king's own coach, the king was much impressed with him, for indeed he was a handsome gentleman, and it was not queer that the king's daughter fell deeply in love with him. Puss in Boots was quite overjoyed to see his plans succeeding so well, and marched on ahead of the carriage.

Meeting some reapers in the field, the cat said to them: "Good people, the king will soon pass this way. If you do not tell him the meadow you are mowing belongs to my lord Marquis of Carabas, you shall be chopped as fine as mincemeat."

When the king came riding by he asked the mowers to whom the meadow they were mowing belonged.

"To my lord Marquis of Carabas!" they answered together, for the threats of Puss in Boots had terrified them.

"A very fine piece of land you have there, my lord marquis," said the king, turning to him.

"You speak the truth, sire," he replied, "for it never fails to bring me a bountiful harvest."

Puss in Boots, going on as before, now came to a field where laborers toiled putting the corn they had cut into great sheaves. To them he said, "Good people, the king will soon pass this way, and if you do not tell him

the princess and a great gentleman of the court were within, had not dared enter. The king was so charmed with the good qualities of my lord Marquis of Carabas and his vast fortune as well, that after he had partaken of the collation, he said to the marquis, "It will be your own fault if you do not soon become my son-in-law, my dear lord Marquis of Carabas!"

So great haste was made and after a short courtship, the princess became the bride of the marquis and they lived happily ever after.

Puss in Boots was made major-domo and wore the most beautiful clothes and twisted his whiskers like a real live lord, and became so great a personage he would not even look at a rat.

Just why he knew how to do all this for his master I do not know, but I think it must have been because he wore boots—don't you?

The Cats and the Monkey

TWO cats stole some cheese and then fell to quarreling about the fair division of the prize. At length they agreed to go to the monkey and let him settle the dispute.

The monkey readily accepted the office of judge. He produced a balance and, breaking the cheese in two, put one piece into each scale.

"Let me see," said he. "Ah!—this lump on the right outweighs the other." And he bit off a considerable piece in order to make it balance.

Now the piece on the left was heavier, and so Judge Monkey took a large bite from that. But that made the piece on the right again heavier. So the judge went on nibbling first from one piece and then from the other.

"Stop! Stop!" cried the cats, who saw their cheese steadily diminishing. "We are satisfied. Let us have the two pieces as they are."

"Not so fast, not so fast!" replied the monkey. "You may be satisfied, but the court is not. What remains is my fee."

Thereupon he crammed the rest of the cheese in his mouth and declared the case settled.

—*Aesop.*

Over in the Meadow

OVER in the meadow,
    In the sand, in the sun,
Lived an old mother-toad
    And her little toady one.
"Wink," said the mother;
    "I wink," said the one;
So she winked and she blinked
    In the sand, in the sun.

Over in the meadow,
    Where the stream runs blue,
Lived an old mother-fish
    And her little fishes two.
"Swim," said the mother;
    "We swim," said the two;
So they swam and they leaped
    Where the stream runs blue.

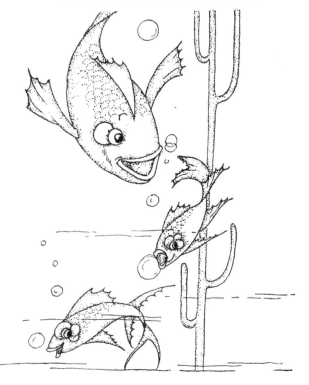

Over in the meadow,
    In a hole in a tree,
Lived an old mother-bluebird
    And her little birdies three.
"Sing," said the mother;
    "We sing," said the three;
So they sang and were glad
    In the hole in the tree.

Over in the meadow,
    In the reeds on the shore,
Lived an old mother-muskrat
    And her little ratties four.
"Dive," said the mother;
    "We dive," said the four;
So they dived and they burrowed
    In the reeds on the shore.

Over in the meadow,
    In a snug beehive,
Lived a mother-honeybee
    And her little bees five;
"Buzz," said the mother;
    "We buzz," said the five;
So they buzzed and they hummed
    In the snug beehive.

Over in the meadow,
    In a nest built of sticks,
Lived a black mother-crow
    And her little crows six.
"Caw," said the mother;
    "We caw," said the six;
So they cawed and they called
    In their nest built of sticks.

Over in the meadow,
    Where the grass is so even,
Lived a gay mother-cricket
    And her little crickets seven.
"Chirp," said the mother;
    "We chirp," said the seven;
So they chirped cheery notes
    In the grass soft and even.

Over in the meadow,
    By the old mossy gate,
Lived a brown mother-lizard
    And her little lizards eight.
"Bask," said the mother;
    "We bask," said the eight;
So they basked in the sun
    On the old mossy gate.

Over in the meadow,
    Where the quiet pools shine,
Lived a green mother-frog
    And her little froggies nine.
"Croak," said the mother;
    "We croak," said the nine;
So they croaked and they splashed
    Where the quiet pools shine.

Over in the meadow,
    In a sly little den,
Lived a gray mother-spider
    And her little spiders ten.
"Spin," said the mother;
    "We spin," said the ten;
So they spun lace webs
    In their sly little den.
        —*Olive A. Wadsworth.*

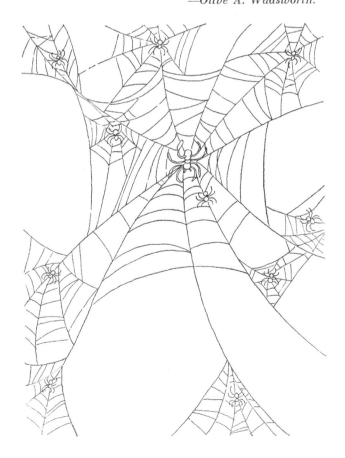

Seven at One Blow

ONE fine day a Tailor was sitting on his bench by the window in very high spirits, sewing away most diligently, and presently up the street came a country woman crying, "Good jams for sale! Good jams for sale!"

This cry sounded nice in the Tailor's ears, and, poking his head out the window, he called out, "Here, my good woman, just bring your jams here!"

The woman mounted the three steps to the Tailor's house with her large basket, and began to open all the pots before him. He looked at them all, and at last said, "These jams seem to me to be very nice, so you may weigh me out two ounces, my good woman." The woman, who hoped to have had a good customer, gave him what he wished, and went off grumbling.

Taking the bread from the cupboard, the Tailor cut himself a slice the size of the whole loaf, and spread the jam upon it. "That will taste very nice," said he; "but before I take a bite, I will just finish this waistcoat." So he put the bread on the table and stitched away, making larger and larger stitches every time for joy.

Meanwhile, the smell of the jam rose to the ceiling, where many flies were sitting, and soon a great swarm of them pitched on the bread.

"Holloa! Who asked you?" exclaimed the Tailor, driving away the uninvited visitors. But the flies came back in greater numbers than before. This put the little man in a great passion and, snatching up a bag of cloth, he brought it down with a merciless swoop upon them. When he raised it again, he counted seven lying dead before him. "What a fellow you are!" said he to himself, astonished at his own bravery. "The whole town must hear of this." In great haste he cut himself out a band, hemmed it, and then put on it in large letters, *Seven at One Blow!*

"Ah," said he, "not one city alone, but the whole world shall hear it!" and his heart danced with joy.

The little Tailor put on the belt, and made ready to travel forth into the wide world. Before he set out, however, he looked about his house to see if there were any thing he could carry with him. He found only an old cheese, which he pocketed, and observing a bird which was caught in the bushes before the door, he captured it and put it in his pocket also. Soon after he set out boldly on his travels. His road led him up a hill, and when he arrived at the top, he found a great Giant sitting there.

The little Tailor went boldly up and said, "Good-day, friend. Truly you sit there and see the whole world stretched out below you. I am on my way thither to seek my fortune. Are you willing to go with me?"

The Giant looked with scorn at the little Tailor and said, "You wretched creature!"

"Perhaps so," replied the Tailor; "but here may be seen what sort of a man I am;" and, unbuttoning his coat, he showed the Giant his belt.

The Giant read, *Seven at One Blow;* and

supposing they were men whom the Tailor had killed, he felt some respect for him. Still he meant to try him. Taking up a pebble, he squeezed it so hard that water dropped out of it. "Do as well as that," said he, "if you have the strength."

"That is child's play," said the Tailor, and diving into his pocket, he pulled out the cheese and squeezed it till the whey ran out of it, and said, "Now I fancy that I have done better than you."

The Giant could not believe it of the little man; so, catching up another pebble, he flung it so high that it went almost out of sight, saying, "There, you pigmy, do that if you can!"

"Well done!" said the Tailor. "But your pebble will fall down again to the ground. I will throw one up which will not come down;" and dipping into his pocket, he took out the bird and threw it into the air. The bird, glad to be free, flew straight up and then far away, and did not come back. "How does that little performance please you, friend?" asked the Tailor.

"You can throw well," replied the Giant. "Now truly we will see if you are able to carry something uncommon." So saying, he took him to a large oak tree, which lay upon the ground, and said, "If you are strong enough, now help me to carry this tree out of the forest."

"With pleasure," replied the Tailor. "You may hold the trunk upon your shoulder and I will lift the boughs and branches."

The Giant took the trunk upon his shoulder, but the Tailor sat down on the branches, and the Giant, who could not look round, was compelled to carry the whole tree and the Tailor also. He being behind the Tailor was very cheerful and laughed at the trick, and presently began to sing as if carrying trees were a trifle.

The Giant, after he had staggered a very short distance with his heavy load, could go no further and called out, "Do you hear? I must drop the tree!"

The Tailor, jumping down, quickly embraced the tree with both arms as if he had been carrying it, and said to the Giant, "Are you such a big fellow, and yet cannot carry a tree?"

Then they traveled on further, and came to a cherry-tree. The Giant seized the top of it where the ripest cherries hung and, bending it down, gave it to the Tailor to hold, telling him to eat the fruit. But the Tailor was far too weak to hold the tree down, and when the Giant let go, the tree flew up into the air, and the Tailor was taken with it. He came down on the other side, unhurt, and the Giant said, "What does that mean? Are you not strong enough to hold that twig?"

"My strength did not fail me," said the Tailor. "Do you imagine that was a hard task for one who has slain seven at one blow? I sprang over the tree because the hunters were shooting down there in the thicket. Jump after me if you can."

The Giant made the attempt, but could not clear the tree, and stuck fast in the branches; so in this affair, too, the Tailor had the advantage.

Then the Giant said, "Since you are such a brave fellow, come with me to my house and stop a night with me."

The Tailor agreed and followed him to the cave. There two other Giants sat by the fire, each with a roast sheep in his hand, of which he was eating.

The Tailor sat down, thinking, "Ah, this is very much more like the world than is my workshop."

Soon the Giant pointed out a bed where he could sleep. The bed, however, was too large for him, so he crept out of it and lay down in a corner.

When midnight came, and the Giant fancied the Tailor would be in a sound sleep, he got up, and taking an iron bar, broke the bed at one stroke, and believed he had thereby given the Tailor his death blow. At dawn the Giants went out into the forest, quite forgetting the Tailor. Presently up he came quite cheerful. The Giants were frightened, and dreading he might kill them all, they ran away in a great hurry.

The Tailor traveled on, always follow-ing his nose, and after he had journeyed a long distance, he came to the courtyard of a royal palace. Feeling very tired, he lay down on the ground and went to sleep. While he lay there people came to look at him and read upon his belt, *Seven at One Blow*. "Ah," said they, "what does this great warrior here?" And they went and told the King.

The King sent one of his courtiers to the Tailor, to beg for his fighting services, if he should be awake. The messenger stopped at the sleeper's side and waited until he stretched out his limbs and unclosed his eyes, and then he told his message.

"Solely for that reason did I come here," said the Tailor. So he was taken away with great honor, and a fine house was appointed him to dwell in.

The courtiers, however, became jealous

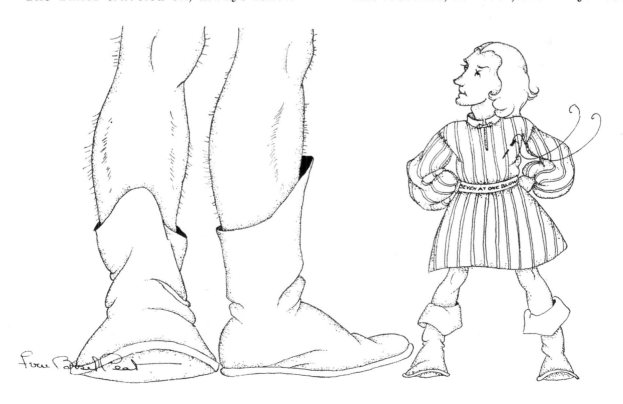

of the Tailor and wished him at the other end of the world. In their anger they determined to resign, and they went all together to the King and asked his permission.

The King was sorry to lose all his devoted servants for the sake of one, and wished he had never seen the Tailor. He dare not, however, dismiss him because he feared the Tailor might kill him and all his subjects, and seat himself on the throne. For a long time he deliberated. Then he sent for the Tailor and told him that, seeing he was so great a hero, he wished to beg a favor of him.

"In a certain forest in my kingdom," said the King, "there are two Giants, who have committed great damage, and no one approaches them without endangering his own life. If you overcome and slay both these Giants, I will give you my only daughter in marriage, and the half of my kingdom for a dowry. A hundred knights shall accompany you, too, in order to render you assistance."

"Ah, that is something for a man like me," thought the Tailor to himself. "A lovely Princess and half a kingdom are not offered to one every day." "Oh, yes," he replied, "I will soon settle these two Giants, and the hundred horsemen are not needed for that purpose; he who kills seven at one blow has no fear of two."

So the little Tailor set out, followed by the hundred knights. When they came to the edge of the forest, he said to them, "You must stay here. I prefer to meet these Giants alone."

Then he ran off into the forest, and after a while he saw the two Giants sound asleep under a tree. The Tailor, bold as a lion, filled both his pockets with stones and climbed up the tree. When he got to the middle of it he crawled along a bough, so that he sat just above the sleepers, and then he let fall one stone after another upon one of them. Awaking at last, the Giant pushed his companion and said, "Why are you hitting me?"

"You have been dreaming," answered the other. "I did not touch you."

So they laid themselves down again, and presently the Tailor threw a stone down upon the other.

"What is that?" he cried. "Why are you knocking me about?"

"I did not touch you. You are dreaming," said the first. So they argued for a few minutes, and then both went to sleep again.

Then the Tailor picked out the largest stone, and threw it with all his strength upon the chest of the first Giant.

"This is too bad!" he exclaimed; and, jumping up like a madman, he fell upon his companion, who considered himself equally injured, and they set to in such good earnest that they rooted up trees and beat one another about until they both fell dead upon the ground.

The Tailor jumped down, saying, "What a piece of luck they did not pull up the tree on which I sat!" He drew his sword, cut a deep wound in the breast of both, and then went to the horsemen and said, "The deed is done. I have given each his death stroke, but it was a tough job, for in their defense they uprooted trees to protect themselves."

"And are you not wounded?" they asked.

"How can you ask me that? They have not injured a hair of my head," replied the little man.

The knights could hardly believe him until, riding into the forest, they found the Giants lying dead, and the uprooted trees around them.

Then the Tailor demanded the promised reward of the King; but he repented of his promise, and began to think of some new plan to shake off the hero.

"Before you receive my daughter and the half of my kingdom," said he, "you must execute another brave deed. In the forest there lives a unicorn that does great damage. You must catch him."

"I fear a unicorn less than I did two Giants! *Seven at One Blow* is my motto," said the Tailor. So he took a rope and an axe and went off to the forest, ordering those who accompanied him to wait on the outskirts. He had not to hunt long, for soon the unicorn approached, and rushed at him as if it would pierce him on the spot.

"Steady! Steady!" he exclaimed. "That is not done so easily;" and, waiting till the animal was close upon him, he sprang nimbly behind a tree. The unicorn, rushing with all its force against the tree, stuck its horn fast in the trunk, and so was a prisoner.

"Now I have got him," said the Tailor; and, coming from behind the tree, he first bound the rope around its neck, and then cutting the horn out of the tree with his axe, he led the unicorn before the King.

The King, however, would not yet deliver the promised reward, and made a third demand. Before marriage, the Tailor should capture a wild boar which did much damage, and he should have the huntsmen to help him.

"With pleasure," was the reply; "it is a mere nothing." To their great joy, he left the huntsmen behind.

As soon as the boar saw the Tailor, it ran at him with gaping mouth and glistening teeth and tried to throw him down on the ground; but our hero sprang into a little chapel which stood near, and out again at a window on the other side in a moment. The boar ran after him but he, skipping around, closed the door behind it and the furious beast was caught.

The Tailor now ordered the huntsmen up, that they might see his prisoner with their own eyes while he presented himself before the King, who was obliged at last to keep his word and surrender his daughter and the half of his kingdom.

So the wedding was celebrated with great magnificence, though with little rejoicing, and out of a Tailor there was made a King.

A short time afterwards the young Queen heard her husband talking in his sleep, and saying, "Boy, make me a coat and then stitch up these trousers, or I will lay the yard-measure over your shoulders!"

In the morning she complained to her father and begged he would free her from her husband who was nothing more than a Tailor.

The King said, "This night leave your chamber-door open. My servants shall stand outside, and when he is asleep they shall come in, bind him, and carry him away to a ship, which shall take him into the wide world."

The wife was pleased with the proposal; but the King's armor-bearer, who had overheard all, went to the young King and revealed the whole plot.

"I will soon put an end to this affair," said the valiant little Tailor.

In the evening they went to bed, and when his wife thought he slept, she got up, opened the door, and laid herself down again.

The Tailor, however, only pretended to sleep, and began to call out in a loud voice, "Boy, make me a coat, and then stitch up these trousers, or I will lay the yard-measure about your shoulders! Seven have I slain with one blow, two Giants have I killed, a unicorn have I led captive, and a wild boar have I caught, and shall I be afraid of those who stand outside my room?"

When the men heard these words, a great fear came over them and they ran away as if wild huntsmen were following them. Afterwards no man dared venture to oppose him.

Thus the Tailor became a King, and so he lived for the rest of his life.

—*Adapted from Grimm.*

SEVEN AT ONE BLOW

The Three Little Pigs

ONCE there was an old mother pig who had three little pigs. She found she did not have enough to keep them, so she sent them out into the world to seek their fortunes.

The first little pig had not gone far when he met a man with a bundle of straw. The little pig said to him: "Please, man, give me that straw to build me a house."

This the man did, and soon the little pig had built a house with it.

Just after the house was built, along came a wolf. He knocked at the door of the little pig's house and said, "Little pig, little pig, let me come in!"

But the little pig answered, "No, no! Not by the hair of my chinny chin chin!"

Then the wolf said, "I'll huff and I'll puff, and I'll blow your house in!"

But the little pig wouldn't let him in, so he huffed and he puffed and he blew the house in—and ate up that little pig.

The second little pig met a man with a bundle of sticks. The little pig said to him: "Please, man, give me those sticks to build me a house."

The man did this, and soon the little pig had built a house with them.

Just after the house was built, along came the wolf. He knocked at the little pig's door and said, "Little pig, little pig, let me come in!"

But the little pig answered: "No, no! Not by the hair of my chinny chin chin!"

Then the wolf said, "I'll huff and I'll puff, and I'll blow your house in!"

So he huffed, and he puffed, and he huffed, and he puffed, and at last he blew the house in—and ate up that little pig.

The third little pig met a man with a load of bricks. The little pig said to him: "Please, man, give me those bricks to build me a house."

This the man did, and soon the little pig had built a house with them.

Just after the house was built, along came the wolf. He knocked at the little pig's door and said: "Little pig, little pig, let me come in!"

But the little pig answered: "No, no! Not by the hair of my chinny chin chin!"

Then the wolf said, "I'll huff and I'll puff and I'll blow your house in!"

So he huffed and he puffed, and he puffed and he huffed, and he huffed, and he puffed, but he couldn't blow this little pig's house in.

When he found that with all his huffing and puffing he could not get this little pig's house down, he said: "Little pig, I know where there is a field of fine turnips."

"Where?" eagerly asked the little pig.

"Over in Mr. Smith's home-field. And if you will be ready tomorrow morning, I will call for you and we will go together and get some for our dinner."

"Thank you," replied the little pig. "I will be ready. What time do you mean to go?"

"Oh, six o'clock."

Now the little pig arose at five o'clock and was back home with his turnips when about six o'clock the wolf came and said: "Little pig, are you ready?"

"Ready?" exclaimed the little pig. "Why, I have been and am back again, and I have a fine pot of turnips ready for my dinner!"

The wolf was very angry, but thinking he would be equal to the little pig, he said: "Little pig, I know where there is a nice apple tree."

"Where?" eagerly asked the little pig.

"Down at Merry Garden," replied the wolf. "And if you will not deceive me, I will come for you at five o'clock tomorrow morning and we will go together and get some apples."

Now the little pig bustled around the next morning at four o'clock. He hoped to get home again before the wolf arrived, but this time he had to go farther, and besides he had to climb the tree to get the apples. Just as he was ready to jump down and

hurry home, he spied the wolf coming. Yes, indeed, the little pig was badly frightened!

The wolf came up under the tree and said: "What, little pig! You here before me? Are they nice apples?"

"Yes, very nice," answered the little pig. "Here, I will throw one down for you."

Now the little pig threw that apple so far that while the wolf was gone after it, he jumped to the ground and ran home.

The next day the wolf came to the little pig's house once more and said: "Little pig, there's a fair over at Shanklin this afternoon. Will you go with me?"

"Oh, yes," replied the little pig. "What time shall I expect you?"

"At three," answered the wolf.

The little pig went off before three, just as usual, got to the fair, bought a butter churn and was going home with it when he spied the wolf coming.

This time the little pig *was* frightened. He could not tell what to do. So he got into the churn to hide and in climbing in, it started to roll round and round. Down the hill it rolled, faster and faster, with the little pig in it. This frightened the wolf so that he ran home, forgetting all about going to the fair at Shanklin.

The next day he went to the little pig's house and told him how frightened he had been by having a great round thing come rolling down the hill past him.

The little pig laughed and said, "Ha, ha! I frightened you that time! I had been to the fair and bought a butter churn and when I saw you coming, I climbed inside and rolled down the hill."

Then the wolf was very angry indeed.

A Color Illustration *(over)*

The mother pig did not have enough
to keep them, so she sent them out
into the world to seek their fortunes.

He vowed he would eat up that little pig—that he would go down the chimney after him.

When the little pig saw what the wolf was about, he made a blazing fire, filled a big pot of water and hung it over the fire. Then just as the wolf was coming down the chimney, he lifted off the lid and in fell the wolf. The little pig quickly popped on the cover again, and had the wolf for supper.

And that is how it came about that this little pig lived happily ever after.

—An English Story.

The Owl and the Pussy Cat

THE Owl and the Pussy-cat went to sea
  In a beautiful pea-green boat:
They took some honey, and plenty of
    money
  Wrapped up in a five-pound note.
The Owl looked up to the stars above,
  And sang to a small guitar,
"O lovely Pussy, O Pussy, my love,
  What a beautiful Pussy you are,
      You are,
      You are!
What a beautiful Pussy you are!"

Pussy said to the Owl, "You elegant fowl,
  How charmingly sweet you sing!
Oh! let us be married; too long we have
    tarried:
  But what shall we do for a ring?"
They sailed away, for a year and a day,
  To the land where the bong tree grows;
And there in a wood a Piggy-wig stood,
  With a ring at the end of his nose,
      His nose,
      His nose,
  With a ring at the end of his nose.

"Dear Pig, are you willing to sell for one shilling
  Your ring?" Said the Piggy, "I will."
So they took it away, and were married next day
  By the Turkey who lives on the hill.
They dined on mince and slices of quince,
  Which they ate with a runcible spoon;
And hand in hand, on the edge of the sand,
  They danced by the light of the moon,
      The moon,
      The moon,
They danced by the light of the moon.

—Edward Lear.

Little Half-Chick

ONCE upon a time in the country called Spain there was a handsome black hen, who had a brood of thirteen chickens. All of them were fine, plump little chicks except the youngest. This one looked just as if he had been cut in two. He had only one leg, and one wing, and one eye; and he had half a head and half a beak.

Now Little Half-Chick proved to be as unlike his brothers and sisters in character as he was in appearance. They were good, obedient chickens, and when the old hen clucked after them they chirped and ran back to her side. But when his mother called Little Half-Chick he ran on, pretending he could not hear because he had only one ear.

As he grew older he became more self-willed and disobedient. One day he strutted up to his mother with the peculiar hop and kick which was his way of walking, and cocking his one eye at her in a very bold way, he said, "Mother, I am tired of this dull farmyard. I'm off to Madrid to see the king."

"To Madrid, Little Half-Chick!" exclaimed his mother. "Why, you silly chick, you would be tired out before you had gone half the distance!"

But Little Half-Chick had made up his mind, and he would not listen to his mother's advice. Scarcely waiting to say good-bye to his family, away he stumped down the high-road that led to Madrid.

"Be sure that you are kind and civil to everyone you meet," his mother called after him.

But he was in such a hurry to be off that he did not wait to answer her, or even to look back.

A little later in the day, as he was taking a short cut through a field, he passed a stream. Now the stream was all choked up so that its waters could not flow freely.

"Oh! Little Half-Chick," it cried, "do come and help me by clearing away these weeds."

"Help you, indeed!" exclaimed Little Half-Chick, tossing his head, and shaking the few feathers in his tail. "I am off to Madrid to see the king." And hoppity-kick, hoppity-kick, away stumped Little Half-Chick.

A little later he came to a fire that had been left in a wood. It was burning very low.

"Oh! Little Half-Chick," cried the fire in a weak, wavering voice, "in a few minutes I shall go quite out unless you put some sticks on me. Do come and help me!"

"Help you, indeed!" answered Little Half-Chick. "Gather sticks for yourself. I am off to Madrid to see the king." And hoppity-kick, hoppity-kick, away stumped Little Half-Chick.

The next morning he passed a large chestnut tree in whose branches the wind was caught.

"Oh! Little Half-Chick," called the wind, "do help me to get free of these branches!"

"It is your own fault for going there," answered Little Half-Chick. "Just shake yourself off. I am off to Madrid to see the king." And hoppity-kick, hoppity-kick, away stumped Little Half-Chick in great glee, for the towers and roofs of Madrid were now in sight.

When he entered the town he saw a splendid house, with soldiers standing before the gates. This he knew must be the king's palace, and he determined to hop to the front gate and wait there until the king came out. But as he was hopping past one of the back windows, the king's cook saw him.

"Here is the very thing I want," he exclaimed, and opening the window, he caught Little Half-Chick and popped him into the broth-pot.

Oh! how wet and clammy the water felt as it went over Little Half-Chick's head, making his feathers cling to his side.

"Water, water!" he cried in despair, "do have pity on me and do not wet me like this."

"Ah! Little Half-Chick," answered the water, "you would not help me when I was a little stream away on the fields. Now you must be punished."

Then the fire began to burn and scald Little Half-Chick.

"Fire, fire! do not scorch me like this; you can't think how it hurts."

"Ah! Little Half-Chick," answered the fire, "you would not help me when I was dying away in the wood. You are being punished."

At last, just when the pain was so great that Little Half-Chick thought he must die, the cook lifted up the lid of the pot to see if the broth was ready for the king's dinner.

"This chicken is quite useless," he cried in horror. "The water has boiled away, and it is burnt to a cinder." And opening the window, he threw Little Half-Chick out into the street.

But the wind caught him up and whirled him through the air so quickly that Little Half-Chick could scarcely breathe.

73

"Oh! wind," at last he gasped out, "if you hurry me along like this you will kill me. Do let me rest a moment, or——" but he was so breathless he could not finish.

"Ah! Little Half-Chick," replied the wind, "when I was caught in the branches of the chestnut tree, you would not help me; you are punished now. You have never obeyed or served anyone. Now that will be changed."

He swirled Little Half-Chick over the roofs of the houses till they reached the highest church in town. There he left him fastened to the top of the steeple.

And if you should go to Madrid today, you would see Little Half-Chick there, perched on his one little leg, with his one little wing drooping at his side, turning this way and that at the command of the wind, serving all the people as a weather vane.

—*A Spanish Story.*

The Fisherman and His Wife

THERE was once a fisherman who lived with his wife in a ditch, close by the sea-side. The fisherman used to go out all day long a-fishing: and one day, as he sat on the shore with his rod, looking at the shining water and watching his line, all on a sudden his float was dragged away deep under the sea: and in drawing it up he pulled a great fish out of the water.

The fish said to him, "Pray, let me live. I am not a real fish; I am an enchanted prince. Put me in the water again, and let me go."

"Oh!" said the man, "you need not make so many words about the matter. I wish to have nothing to do with a fish that can talk; so swim away as soon as you please." Then he put him back into the water, and the fish darted straight down to the bottom, and left a long streak of blood behind him.

When the fisherman went home to his wife in the ditch, he told her how he had caught a great fish, and how it had told him it was an enchanted prince, and that on hearing it speak, he had let it go again.

"Did you not ask it for anything?" said the wife.

"No," said the man; "what should I ask for?"

"Ah!" said the wife, "we live very wretchedly here in this nasty stinking ditch; do go back and tell the fish we want a little cottage."

The fisherman did not much like the business; however, he went to the sea, and when he came there, the water looked all yellow and green. And he stood at the water's edge, and said,

"O man of the sea!
Come listen to me,
For Alice my wife,
The plague of my life,
Hath sent me to beg a boon of thee!"

Then the fish came swimming to him and asked, "Well, what does she want?"

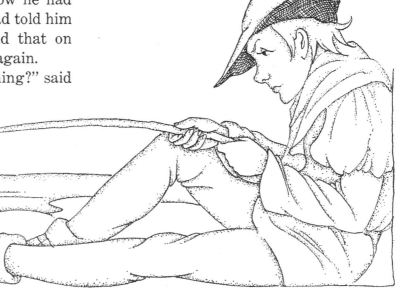

"Ah!" answered the fisherman, "my wife says that when I had caught you, I ought to have asked you for something before I let you go again. She does not like living any longer in the ditch, and wants a little cottage."

"Go home, then," said the fish; "she is in the cottage already."

So the man went home, and saw his wife standing at the door of a cottage.

"Come in, come in," said she. "Is not this much better than the ditch?"

And there was a parlor, and a bedchamber, and a kitchen; and behind the cottage there was a little garden with all sorts of flowers and fruits, and a courtyard full of ducks and chickens.

"Ah!" said the fisherman, "how happy we shall live!"

"We shall try to do so at least," said his wife.

Everything went right for a week or two, and then one day Dame Alice said, "Husband, there is not room enough in this cottage, and both the courtyard and the garden are a great deal too small. I should like to have a large stone castle to live in. So go to the fish again, and tell him to give us a castle."

"Wife," said the fisherman, "I don't like to go to him again, for perhaps he will be angry; we ought to be content with the cottage."

"Nonsense!" said the wife. "He will do it very willingly; go along and try."

The fisherman went, but his heart was very heavy; and when he came to the sea, it looked blue and gloomy, though it was quite calm. He went close to it and said,

"O man of the sea!
  Come listen to me,
  For Alice my wife,
  The plague of my life,
  Hath sent me to beg a boon of thee!"

"Well, what does she want now?" asked the fish.

"Ah!" said the man very sorrowfully, "my wife wants to live in a stone castle."

"Go home, then," said the fish; "she is standing at the door of it already."

So away went the fisherman, and found his wife standing before a great castle.

"See," said she, "is not this grand?"

With that they went into the castle together, and found a great many servants there, and the rooms all richly furnished and full of golden chairs and tables; and behind the castle was a garden, and a wood half a mile long, full of sheep, and goats, and hares, and deer; and in the courtyard were stables and cow-houses.

"Well!" said the man, "now we will live contented and happy in this beautiful castle for the rest of our lives."

"Perhaps we may," said the wife; "but let us consider and sleep upon it before we make up our minds;" so they went to bed.

The next morning, when Dame Alice awoke, it was broad daylight, and she jogged the fisherman with her elbow, and said, "Get up, husband, and bestir yourself, for we must be king of all the land."

"Wife, wife," said the man, "why should we wish to be king? I will not be king."

"Then I will," said Alice.

"But, wife," answered the fisherman, "how can you be king? The fish cannot make you a king."

"Husband," said she, "say no more about it, but go and try; I will be king!"

So the man went away, quite sorrowful to think that his wife should want to be king. The sea looked a dark-grey color, and was covered with foam as he cried out,

"O man of the sea!
Come listen to me,
For Alice my wife,
The plague of my life,
Hath sent me to beg a boon of thee!"

"Well, what would she have now?" asked the fish.

"Alas!" said the man, "my wife wants to be king."

"Go home," said the fish; "she is king already."

Then the fisherman went home, and as he came close to the palace, he saw a troop of soldiers, and heard the sound of drums and trumpets; and when he entered in, he saw his wife sitting on a high throne of gold and diamonds, with a golden crown upon her head; and on each side of her stood six beautiful maidens, each a head taller than the other.

"Well, wife," said the fisherman, "are you king?"

"Yes," said she, "I am king."

And when he had looked at her for a long time, he said, "Ah, wife! what a fine thing it is to be king! Now we shall never have anything more to wish for."

"I don't know how that may be," said she; "never is a long time. I am king, 'tis true, but I begin to be tired of it, and I think I should like to be emperor."

"Alas, wife! why should you wish to be emperor?" said the fisherman.

"Husband," said she, "go to the fish; I say I will be emperor."

"Ah, wife!" replied the fisherman, "the fish cannot make an emperor, and I should not like to ask for such a thing."

"I am king," said Alice, "and you are my slave, so go directly!"

So the fisherman was obliged to go; and he muttered as he went along, "This will come to no good. It is too much to ask, the fish will be tired at last, and then we shall repent of what we have done."

He soon arrived at the sea, and the water was quite black and muddy, and a mighty whirlwind blew over it; but he went to the shore and said,

"O man of the sea!
  Come listen to me,
  For Alice my wife,
  The plague of my life,
  Hath sent me to beg a boon of thee!"

"What would she have now?" asked the fish.

"Ah!" said the fisherman, "she wants to be emperor."

"Go home," said the fish; "she is emperor already."

So he went home again; and as he came near, he saw his wife sitting on a very lofty throne made of solid gold, with a great crown on her head full two yards high, and on each side of her stood her guards and attendants in a row, each one smaller than the other, from the tallest giant down to a little dwarf no bigger than my finger. And before her stood princes and dukes and earls: and the fisherman went up to her and said, "Wife, are you emperor?"

"Yes," said she, "I am emperor."

"Ah!" said the man, as he gazed upon her, "what a fine thing it is to be emperor!"

"Husband," said the woman, "why should we stay at being emperor? I will be pope next."

"Oh, wife, wife!" said he, "how can you be pope? There is but one pope at a time in Christendom."

"Husband," said she, "I will be pope this very day."

"But," replied the husband, "the fish cannot make you pope."

"What nonsense!" said she. "If he can make an emperor, he can make a pope. Go and try him."

So the fisherman went. But when he came to the shore, the wind was raging, and the sea was tossed up and down like boiling water, and the ships were in the greatest distress and danced upon the waves most fearfully. In the middle of the sky there was a little blue, but towards the south it was all red as if a dreadful storm was rising. At this the fisherman was terribly frightened, and trembled so that his knees knocked together: but he went to the shore and said,

"O man of the sea!
  Come listen to me,
  For Alice my wife,
  The plague of my life,
  Hath sent me to beg a boon of thee!"

"What does she want now?" asked the fish.

"Ah!" said the fisherman, "my wife wants to be pope."

"Go home," said the fish; "she is pope already."

Then the fisherman went home, and found his wife sitting on a throne that was two miles high; and she had three great crowns on her head, and around stood all the pomp and power of the Church; and on each side were two rows of burning lights, of all sizes, the greatest as high as the highest and biggest tower in the world, and the least no larger than a small rushlight.

"Wife," said the fisherman as he looked at all this grandeur, "are you pope?"

"Yes," said she, "I am pope."

"Well, wife," replied he, "it is a grand thing to be pope; and now you must be content, for you can be nothing greater."

"I will consider of that," said the wife.

Then they went to bed: but Dame Alice could not sleep all night for thinking what she should be next. At last morning came, and the sun rose.

"Ha!" thought she, as she looked at it through the window, "cannot I prevent the sun rising?"

At this she was very angry, and she wakened her husband, and said, "Husband, go to the fish and tell him I want to be lord of the sun and moon."

The fisherman was half asleep, but the thought frightened him so much that he started and fell out of bed.

"Alas, wife!" said he, "cannot you be content to be pope?"

"No," said she. "I am very uneasy, and cannot bear to see the sun and moon rise without my leave. Go to the fish directly."

Then the man went trembling for fear; and as he was going down to the shore, a dreadful storm arose, so that the trees and the rocks shook; and the heavens became black, and the lightning played, and the thunder rolled; and you might have seen in the sea great black waves like mountains with a white crown of foam upon them; and the fisherman said,

"O man of the sea!
Come listen to me,
For Alice my wife,
The plague of my life,
Hath sent me to beg a boon of thee!"

"What does she want now?" asked the fish.

"Ah!" said he, "she wants to be lord of the sun and moon."

"Go home," said the fish, "to your ditch again!"

And there they live to this very day.
—*The Brothers Grimm.*

Once There Was a Kitty

ONCE there was a kitty,
    Kitty white as snow.
In a barn he used to frolic
    A long time ago.

In that barn there was a mousie
    Ran to and fro.
But the kit caught little mousie
    A long time ago.

Two black eyes had little kitty,
    Black as a crow.
And they spied the little mousie
    A long time ago.

Four soft paws had little kitty,
    Paws soft as tow.
And they caught the little mousie
    A long time ago.

Nine pearl teeth had little kitty,
    All in a row.
And they bit the little mousie
    A long time ago.

When the kit bit little mousie,
    Mousie cried out, "Oh!"
But the mouse got away from kitty
    A long time ago.
—*Old Verse.*

Three Little Kittens
They Lost Their Mittens

Three little kittens they lost their mittens,
    And they began to cry,
    "Oh! mammy dear,
    We sadly fear
    Our mittens we have lost!"
"What! lost your mittens, you naughty
    kittens!
    Then you shall have no pie!"
       Miew, miew, miew, miew,
       Miew, miew, miew, miew.

The three little kittens they found their
    mittens,
    And they began to cry,
    "Oh! mammy dear,
    See here, see here!
    Our mittens we have found!"
"What! found your mittens, you little
    kittens,
    Then you shall have some pie!"
       Purr, purr, purr, purr,
       Purr, purr, purr, purr.

The three little kittens put on their mittens,
    And soon ate up their pie;
    "Oh! mammy dear,
    We greatly fear
    Our mittens we have soiled!"
"What! soiled your mittens, you naughty
    kittens!"
    Then they began to sigh,
       Miew, miew, miew, miew,
       Miew, miew, miew, miew.

The three little kittens they washed their
    mittens,
    And hung them up to dry;
    "Oh! mammy dear,
    Look here, look here,
    Our mittens we have washed!"
"What! washed your mittens, you darling
    kittens!
    But I smell a rat close by!"
       Rush! hush! miew, miew,
       Miew, miew, miew, miew.

A Color Illustration *(over)*

"Oh! mammy dear,
See here, see here!
Our mittens we have found!"

Lambikin

ONCE upon a time there was a wee, wee Lambikin, who frolicked about on his little tottery legs, and enjoyed himself amazingly. Now one day he set off to visit his Granny, and was jumping with joy to think of all the good things he should get from her, when whom should he meet but a Jackal, who looked at the tender young morsel and said: "Lambikin! Lambikin! I'll eat you!"

But Lambikin only gave a little frisk, and said:

> "To Granny's house I go,
>   Where I shall fatter grow,
>   Then you can eat me so."

The Jackal thought this reasonable, and let Lambikin pass.

By and by he met a Vulture, and the Vulture, looking at the tender morsel before him, said: "Lambikin! Lambikin! I'll eat you!"

But Lambikin only gave a little frisk, and said:

> "To Granny's house I go,
>   Where I shall fatter grow,
>   Then you can eat me so."

The Vulture thought this reasonable, and let Lambikin pass.

And by and by he met a Tiger, and then he met a Wolf, and a Dog, and an Eagle; and all these, when they saw the tender little morsel, said: "Lambikin! Lambikin! I'll eat you!"

But to all of them Lambikin replied, with a little frisk:

> "To Granny's house I go,
>   Where I shall fatter grow,
>   Then you can eat me so."

At last he reached his Granny's house, and said, all in a great hurry, "Granny dear, I've promised to get very fat; so, as people ought to keep their promises, please put me into the corn-bin at once."

So his Granny said he was a good boy, and put him into the corn-bin, and there the greedy little Lambikin stayed for seven days, and ate, and ate, and ate, until he could scarcely waddle, and his Granny said he was fat enough for anything, and must go home. But cunning little Lambikin said that would never do, for some animal would be sure to eat him on the way back, he was so plump and tender.

"I'll tell you what you must do," said Master Lambikin; "you must make a little drumikin out of the skin of my little brother who died, and then I can sit inside and trundle along nicely, for I'm as tight as a drum myself."

So his Granny made a nice little drumikin out of his brother's skin, with the wool inside, and Lambikin curled himself up snug and warm in the middle, and trundled away gaily. Soon he met with the Eagle, who called out:

"Drumikin! Drumikin!
Have you seen Lambikin?"

And Mr. Lambikin, curled up in his soft warm nest, replied:

"Fallen into the fire, and so will you.
On, little Drumikin! Tum-pa, tum-too!"

"How very annoying!" sighed the Eagle, thinking regretfully of the tender morsel he had let slip.

Meanwhile Lambikin trundled along, laughing to himself, and singing:

"Tum-pa, tum-too;
Tum-pa, tum-too!"

Every animal and bird he met asked him the same question:

"Drumikin! Drumikin!
Have you seen Lambikin?"

And to each of them the little sly-boots replied:

"Fallen into the fire, and so will you.
On, little Drumikin! Tum-pa, tum-too;
Tum-pa, tum-too; Tum-pa, tum-too!"

Then they all sighed to think of the tender little morsel they had let slip.

At last the Jackal came limping along, for all his sorry looks as sharp as a needle, and he too called out:

"Drumikin! Drumikin!
Have you seen Lambikin?"

And Lambikin, curled up in his snug little nest, replied gaily:

"Fallen into the fire, and so will you.
On, little Drumikin! Tum-pa——"

But he never got any farther, for the Jackal recognized his voice at once, and cried: "Hullo! You've turned yourself inside out, have you? Just you come out of that!"

Whereupon he tore open Drumikin and gobbled up Lambikin.

—*East Indian Tale.*

Mother Holle

THERE was once a widow who had two daughters, one of whom was beautiful and industrious and the other ugly and lazy. She behaved most kindly, however, to the ugly one, because she was her own daughter; and made the other do all the hard work, and live like a kitchen-maid. The poor maiden was forced out daily on the high-road, and had to sit by a well and spin so much that the blood ran from her fingers.

Once it happened that her spindle became quite covered with blood, so, kneeling down by the well, she tried to wash it off, but unhappily it fell out of her hands into the water. She ran crying to her stepmother and told her misfortune, but she scolded her terribly and behaved very cruelly, and at last said, "Since you have let your spindle fall in, you must yourself fetch it out again!"

Then the maiden went back and in her distress of mind she jumped into the well to fetch the spindle out. As she fell, she lost all consciousness, and when she came to herself again, she found she was in a beautiful meadow, where the sun was shining and many thousands of flowers were blooming around her.

She got up and walked along till she came to a baker's, where the oven was full of bread, which cried out, "Draw me, draw me, or I shall be burned. I have been baked long enough." So she went up, and taking the bread-peel, drew out one loaf after the other.

Then she walked on farther, and came to an apple tree, whose fruit hung very thick, and which exclaimed, "Shake us, shake us; we apples are all ripe!" So she shook the tree till the apples fell down like rain, and when none were left on, she gathered them all together in a heap, and went farther.

At last she came to a cottage, out of which an old woman was peeping, who had such very large teeth that the maiden was frightened and ran away. The old woman, however, called her back, saying, "What are you afraid of, my child? Stop with me: if you will put all things in order in my house, then shall all go well with you. Only you must take care that you make my bed well, and shake it tremendously, so that the feathers fly; then it snows upon earth. I am Old Mother Holle."

As the old woman spoke so kindly, the maiden took courage and consented to engage in her service. Now everything made her very contented, and she always shook the bed so industriously that the feathers blew down like flakes of snow. Therefore her life was a happy one, and there were no evil words; and she had roast and baked meat every day.

For some time she remained with the old woman; but all at once she became very sad and did not herself know what was the matter. At last she found she was homesick and, although she fared a thousand times better than when she was at home, still she longed to go. So she said to her mistress, "I wish to go home, and if it does not go so well with me below as up here, I must return."

The mistress replied, "It appeared to me that you wanted to go home, and since you have served me so truly, I will fetch you up again myself."

So saying, she took her by the hand and led her before a great door, which she undid. And when the maiden was just beneath it, a great shower of gold fell upon her, and a great deal stuck to her so that she was covered over and over with gold.

"That you must have for your industry," said the old woman, giving her the spindle which had fallen into the well.

Thereupon the door was closed, and the maiden found herself upon the earth, not far from her mother's house. As she came into the court, the cock sat upon the house and called,

"Cock-a-doodle-doo!
Our golden maid's come home again."

Then she went in to her mother, and because she was so covered with gold, she was well received.

The maiden related all that had happened. And when the mother heard how she had come by these great riches, she wished her ugly, lazy daughter to try her luck. So she was forced to sit down by the well and spin; and in order that her spindle might become bloody, she pricked her finger by running a thorn into it. Then, throwing the spindle into the well, she jumped in after it. Like the other maiden, she came upon the beautiful meadow, and traveled along the same path.

When she arrived at the baker's, the bread called out, "Draw me out, draw me out, or I shall be burned. I have been baked long enough."

But she answered, "I have no wish to make myself dirty about you," and so went on.

Soon she came to the apple tree, which called out, "Shake me, shake me; my apples are all quite ripe."

But she answered, "You do well to come

to me; perhaps one will fall on my head likewise;" and so she went on farther.

When she came to Old Mother Holle's house, she was not afraid of the teeth for she had been warned, and so she engaged herself to her.

The first day she set to work in earnest, was very industrious and obeyed her mistress in all she said to her, for she thought about the gold which she would present to her. On the second day, however, she began to idle; on the third, still more so; and then she would not get up of a morning. She did not make the beds, either, as she ought, and the feathers did not fly. So the old woman got tired and dismissed her from her service, which pleased the lazy one very well for she thought, "Now the gold shower will come." Her mistress led her to the door, but when she was beneath it, instead of gold, a tubful of pitch was poured down upon her.

"That is the reward of your service," said Old Mother Holle, and shut the door.

Then came Lazy-bones home, but she was quite covered with pitch; and the cock upon the house when he saw her cried,

"Cock-a-doodle-doo!
Our dirty maid's come home again."

But the pitch stuck to her, and as long as she lived would never come off.

—*The Brothers Grimm.*

On New Year's Day in the Morning

I SAW three ships come sailing by,
Come sailing by, come sailing by;
I saw three ships come sailing by,
On New Year's Day in the morning.

And what do you think was in them then?
Was in them then, was in them then?
And what do you think was in them then?
On New Year's Day in the morning.

Three pretty girls were in them then,
Were in them then, were in them then.
Three pretty girls were in them then,
On New Year's Day in the morning.

One could whistle, and one could sing,
And one could play the violin—
Such joy was there at my wedding,
On New Year's Day in the morning.

The Town Mouse and the Country Mouse

ONCE upon a time the country mouse invited her cousin, the town mouse, out to take dinner with her. When they sat down to eat, the town mouse looked disdainfully at the meal.

"What is the matter, cousin?" asked the country mouse. "You are eating nothing at all."

"I am not used to such poor fare," answered the town mouse. "Do you never have anything besides dry corn, and nuts, and roots?"

"No," said the country mouse. "But I like them very well, though they are not rich fare. What do you have, cousin, at your town home?"

"Tomorrow you shall come and have dinner with me, and I will show you," replied the town mouse.

So on the next day the country mouse scampered across the fields to town and to the elegant house where her cousin lived. When she got there she was very hungry indeed.

"Now be very quiet," said the town mouse, "and we will go up to the kitchen and have a feast."

Just as they had crept out of the hole in the wall, the town mouse heard a step. She rushed back into the hole, calling her cousin to follow quickly.

"What's the matter?" asked the country mouse.

"That's the cook. We mustn't let her see us or she would soon make an end of both of us."

When all was quiet, they slipped back into the kitchen and, sniffing the air, the town mouse led the way straight to the shelf where there was a nice new cheese. She began nibbling greedily.

"We must hurry," she said, "or the cook will be back before we are through."

The country mouse saw a smaller piece of cheese that was easier for her to reach,

and had just touched her tooth to it when the town mouse cried out, "Stop! Stop!"

The country mouse jumped back just as something went snap! Trembling with fright, she turned to her cousin. "What was that?"

"Come," said the town mouse, "we must

A Color Illustration *(over)*

The town mouse began eating quickly,
but the country mouse kept looking
nervously around.

get back in our hole for a while. That was a trap and the cook may have heard it. If she did, she will be in to see what it caught. You must never touch small bits of food lying around where it may be gotten easily. It may be a trap, as this was, or it may be poisoned."

The poor little country mouse said nothing, but lay shivering until her cousin thought that it was safe to go out again.

"I saw some cake on the table," said the town mouse. "Let us try that, now we have had our cheese. And don't forget to watch out for the cat!"

"But I have had no cheese," thought the country mouse. "And how am I to watch out for the cat?" However, she said nothing and followed her cousin closely.

The town mouse began eating quickly but the country mouse kept looking nervously around and had scarcely swallowed a crumb when the town mouse leaped down from the table crying, "Quick! the cat!"

The country mouse scampered after her and just reached the hole in time to escape the cat's wicked claws.

"Now it won't be safe to go back there," said the town mouse. "We will slip around to the storehouse and finish our dinner. But be sure to look out for the dog!"

"You may go," said the country mouse, "but I will not. I have eaten scarcely a mouthful, and three times already I have been in danger of my life. I would rather have simple fare and peace of mind than elegant fare and a troubled mind."

And off she trudged to her little nest in the corner of the field

—An English Story.

Snow-White and Rose-Red

IN THE garden in front of a little cottage grew two rose-trees. One bore white roses; the other red. Here a widow lived, and because her two daughters were so much like the rose-trees, she called one Snow-white and the other Rose-red. Snow-white helped the mother with the work, while Rose-red chased butterflies and gathered the flowers in the fields.

One evening in winter when a snow storm was sending the flakes whirling through the air, the mother said, "Snow-white, close the shutters while Rose-red fixes the fire, and then we'll sit and read."

Beside them on the floor lay their pet lamb, and on the high back of the mother's chair perched their white dove, its head under its wing.

Soon there was a knock at the door, and the mother said, "Open the door, Rose-red. Perhaps a traveler seeks shelter."

But when the door swung open, there stood a bear. Rose-red screamed as he poked his black head through the doorway, the pet lamb bleated in fright, and the dove flapped its wings, while Snow-white clung to Rose-red in dismay. But the bear said, "Don't be afraid. I am half frozen and wish to warm myself at your fire."

"Come in, poor bear!" spoke up the mother. "Daughters, the bear will not hurt you; he's both good and honest."

Gradually Snow-white and Rose-red lost their fear, and when the bear asked them to beat the snow out of his fur, they thought it great fun to brush him until his coat was thoroughly dry. Indeed, they grew to be great friends with the bear, tugging at his fur, pummelling him and rolling him over the floor. When the play went too far, the bear would say:

> "Snow-white and Rose-red,
>   Don't beat your lover dead."

All winter long the bear came to the cottage every evening and would play with the children. In fact, the door was never closed until he had come in.

One morning as spring was coming, the bear said, "Snow-white, I must go away and not come again the whole summer long."

"Oh, bear dear, where are you going, and why?" asked Snow-white.

"To the woods. There I have treasure I must protect from the wicked dwarfs. When the warm spring sun softens the earth, they come through to steal what they can."

So Snow-white unbarred the cottage door, and as the bear went out she thought she caught a glimpse of glittering gold under his fur as it caught on the latch. But she was not sure.

A short time after this Snow-white and Rose-red went to the woods to gather fagots for the fire and came upon a great tree that had fallen. They saw something jumping up and down on the long trunk and when they came nearer, found it was a dwarf with a wrinkled face and a beard a yard long. He glared at them and screamed, "What are you standing there for? Can't you come and help me?"

"What are you doing?" asked Rose-red.

"Stupid!" shouted the dwarf. "I wanted to split this tree trunk to get chips for our fire. I was driving in a wedge when it sprang out and the tree closed so quickly it caught my beautiful white beard. I am stuck fast and here you both just stand and laugh!" and the more he talked, the more angry he grew.

Snow-white and Rose-red hurried to his aid but work as they would they couldn't get the beard loose.

"I will run and bring somebody," said Rose-red at last, at which the dwarf shouted:

"You blockheads! What's the use of calling anyone else? Have you no better plan?"

"Just be a little patient," said Snow-white calmly, and taking her scissors out of her pocket, she cut off the end of the beard.

When the dwarf found himself free, he quickly seized a bag of gold hidden among the roots of the tree, slung it over his shoulder and hastened off, mumbling, "Wretches they are to cut off a piece of my splendid beard!"

It was not long after this that Snow-white and Rose-red went to the brook to catch some fish for their dinner. As they reached the stream, they saw what they supposed was a large grasshopper, but as they ran after it, they saw it was the old dwarf.

"What are you going to do?" asked Rose-red.

"Surely you are not going to jump into the river?" said Snow-white.

"No such fool as that!" snapped the dwarf. "Don't you see that fish is trying to drag me in?"

True enough! The dwarf had been sitting on the bank fishing, and the wind had entangled his beard and line.

When the big fish took his hook, the dwarf was unable to land him, and in spite of his efforts, he was being drawn closer and closer to the water's edge.

The girls found beard and line in a hopeless tangle, and so once more Snow-white took out her scissors and cut the beard to free the dwarf. But he stamped around in a temper, shouting, "You call yourselves polite, do you, to disfigure me so? It was bad enough the first time you cut it off, but now you have cut off the best of it!" Then he lifted up a bag of pearls and disappeared behind a stone.

Not long after this the two sisters went to the village and saw a huge bird circling above them. As it settled on a rock close by, they ran forward to find the eagle had pounced on the dwarf they had seen twice before and would have carried him away had not the sisters fought off the bird.

"Useless creatures you are!" he shouted ungratefully. "See, my coat is torn into shreds!" Then taking up a bag of precious stones, he disappeared under the rock.

This time the girls did not wonder at his temper, but they were surprised when they came home to find him pouring his precious stones on the ground. The sun made the gems sparkle so that the girls stood gazing at them admiringly. When he discovered them, he screamed in a rage, "Why stand gaping so?"

Just then a black bear trotted out of the woods. He growled so the dwarf leaped up in fright, but before he could reach his retreat under the rocks, the bear was upon him.

"Dear Bear, spare me!" he pleaded. "I'll give you all my treasure! A poor little fellow like me would give you no pleasure.

See, those two wicked girls would make tender eating for you!" But the bear gave the dwarf one blow with his paw and he fell dead.

"Snow - white! Rose - red! Don't run away!" called the bear, and suddenly there stood a handsome man, all dressed in gold. "I am the king's son," said he. "I was doomed by that miserable dwarf who stole my treasure to roam as a bear until his death freed me."

Then Snow-white married the prince and Rose-red married his brother. And that is how it came that all the years their mother lived, she had two rose-trees near the window, one bearing the finest of red roses, the other the sweetest of white ones.

The Hare and the Hedgehog

IT WAS a sunny morning in spring and Mr. Hedgehog was out for an early stroll so that he might have a good appetite for the breakfast his wife was cooking. He was just looking over a newly-plowed field when Mr. Hare came by.

"Good-morning," said Mr. Hedgehog very civilly.

"Good-morning," said Mr. Hare. "Where are you going?"

"I am going for a walk," answered Mr. Hedgehog.

"For a walk? With those short, bandy legs?" said Mr. Hare scornfully.

"My legs are as good as yours," retorted Mr. Hedgehog, "and to prove it I'll run you a race."

"All right," said Mr. Hare. "We'll each run down one of these furrows, and if you beat me to the other end, I'll give you a gold piece."

"Agreed!" cried Mr. Hedgehog. "But my wife is waiting breakfast on me and I must go home and eat. Besides, I am a little weak for want of food. Meet me here in an hour."

Mr. Hare made no objection, so home trotted Mr. Hedgehog. He knew he could not beat Mr. Hare in a race, but he had a plan to teach him a lesson. Throwing open his door, he called, "Wife, wife, leave the breakfast and come quick! I am to race with Mr. Hare."

"With Mr. Hare!" exclaimed the surprised Mrs. Hedgehog. "Are you losing your wits?"

"Now listen," said Mr. Hedgehog, and he told her his plan.

How she did laugh! Then they set out together to the far end of the field where Mrs. Hedgehog remained. Mr. Hedgehog scampered back to the other end and arrived just as Mr. Hare hopped up.

"All ready?" asked Mr. Hare.

"All ready!" answered Mr. Hedgehog.

So they each took a furrow. The dirt was piled so high between them that they couldn't see each other.

"When I count three," shouted Mr. Hare, "we start."

"All right," shouted Mr. Hedgehog.

So Mr. Hare counted, "One, two, three!" and he was off like the wind.

When he arrived at the end of his furrow, a hedgehog popped up in the other furrow, and said, "I am here already."

Mr. Hare was astonished. "There must be some mistake," he cried. "We will have to run again."

And, "One, two, three!" he was racing back up the furrow.

When Mr. Hare reached the starting point, Mr. Hedgehog raised up from his furrow and cried, "Here I am already."

But Mr. Hare couldn't believe it this time either and must race again. The same thing happened as before.

Mr. Hare ran up and down that furrow seventy-three times and each time he got to the end, a hedgehog raised up from the other furrow and cried out, "I am here already."

Mr. Hare started down the seventy-fourth time but stopped in the middle, tired out. He had to lie down and rest.

Mr. Hedgehog collected his gold piece, remarking, "Long wits are better than long legs."

Then he took his wife and skipped off for home.

When Mr. Hare raised up and saw them crossing the field, looking exactly alike, he understood Mr. Hedgehog's remark, and was so ashamed of his foolishness that he slipped home the back way, determined never to mention long legs again.

Mr. and Mrs. Hedgehog almost split their sides laughing at the joke on Mr. Hare. And what an appetite for breakfast Mr. Hedgehog had!

—*English Tale.*